S0-AXT-608

JODY

DEBORAH KENT

SCHOLASTIC INC.
New York Toronto London Auckland Sydney

Cover Photo by Owen Brown

ISBN 0-590-41065-2

12 11 10 9 8 7 6 5 4 3 2   9/8 01 2/9

Printed in the U.S.A.   01

JODY

A Wishing Star Book

WISHING STAR TITLES
FROM SCHOLASTIC

ONE

From the moment I opened my mouth to read the first line I knew it just wasn't right. Practicing in front of the mirror last night I'd recognized Elizabeth Barrett's smile, the lift of her shoulders, the stubborn set of her jaw once her mind was made up. I'd spoken with her voice, full of wit and laughter and tenderness.

But now, when it really mattered, my throat caught at the words and I struggled to make them clear. My head pounded. The lines swam before my eyes, and once I even missed a cue. Today I wasn't Elizabeth Barrett. I was just an ordinary high school student stumbling through a wilderness of half-remembered lines.

It was a relief when Mrs. Ikeda finally said, "Okay, Jody, thanks. Now who else wants to try out for Elizabeth?"

Mark waited for me in the third row. He whispered something as I sank into the seat next to him and I leaned closer to catch, " . . . great! Outstanding!"

I shook my head. "I'm just glad it's over."

"No, I mean it." Mark's voice crept up above a whisper and I leaned back a little. "Sure you were a little nervous — everybody's nervous at a tryout. But once you got into it you were fine. I bet you'll get the part."

"Hey, thanks. You really think so?" I leafed back through my script and reread some of Elizabeth's lines. I wanted to believe Mark was right. Maybe I hadn't done so badly after all. It was hard to tell anything through this throbbing behind my eyes.

By now a brown-haired tenth-grader, Barbara something, had taken my place on the stage. Mark and I fell silent and listened to her clear, precise reading. I had to admit to myself that she was pretty good.

Mark nudged me. "She's lifeless," he said loyally. "No energy."

But Mrs. Ikeda didn't give a hint of how she felt about any of us when Barbara's turn was over. "Anyone else?" she asked. Nobody filled in the silence so she went on, "I'll post the list of the cast on the bulletin board outside the main office first thing tomorrow morning. The first rehearsal will be Wednesday at seven-thirty, and I mean seven-thirty sharp."

If you didn't know her you might get the impression that Mrs. Ikeda was one of those really strict by-the-rules teachers. I'd been a little afraid of her last spring when I helped backstage with the Drama Club's production of *Our Hearts Were Young and Gay*. But by the end of the first rehearsal her smile had sparkled through the businesslike veneer and I saw how young and

2

pretty and full of enthusiasm she really was. All of us wanted to do our best for her.

One night the girl who played the lead missed a rehearsal, so I filled in for her, reading her lines on stage. I was thrilled when Mrs. Ikeda came up to me afterward and said she hoped I would try out for a part in the next Drama Club play. I'd dreamed for months ever since about learning lines and gestures, about discovering all the subtleties the playwright had woven into my character.

Now I avoided glancing toward Mrs. Ikeda as Mark and I left the auditorium. I wanted to believe Mark, wanted to believe that I had done fine and would be given the part of Elizabeth in *The Barretts of Wimpole Street*. But I wasn't quite myself today. I felt I'd disappointed Mrs. Ikeda. I knew I'd disappointed myself.

Out in the corridor Mark turned and gave me a long searching look. "You feel all right, Jody? You look kind of funny."

"Around sixth period I started getting a headache. And I've got a little sore throat, too."

"You do sound sort of hoarse," Mark said. "When you were reading up there I thought you just did that to sound older."

"Oh, did I?" I asked. "Sound older, I mean?"

"You sounded fine," Mark repeated. "I'll be seeing your name in lights one of these days."

"Well," I said, laughing, "if that ever happens you can be my public relations man, okay?"

My head had begun to pound with each step I took. But it was better not to think about it. I hated to complain about things like that. I was never one of those helpless, fragile girls who got upset about every little scrape and bruise. Mark was always so sympathetic, but I didn't need him to make a fuss over me. If I had any talent as an actress, I told myself, I ought to be able to act like a girl who didn't have a splitting headache.

On the way to the front door we passed the main office and on the opposite wall hung the bulletin board. I paused and stared at it, a patchwork of notices about club meetings and contributions to the school magazine. Tomorrow morning would I rush over here to read the news, or would my feet grow heavy and reluctant? Would I put off knowing the truth for as long as I could?

A familiar voice at my back swept my questions aside. "Hey, Jody! Mark! How'd everything go? Jody, did you get the part or what?" And my best friend, Nancy Kowalski, caught up with us as we started down the hall again to the foyer.

"I don't know," I began. "It was kind of —"

"Somebody told me it's about a couple of poets or something. Sounds a little weird. How do they come up with all these weird plays all the time?" Nancy demanded.

"Oh, it's a really good play. I think you'll like it," I said. We pushed through the heavy double doors and out into the bitter January afternoon. "It's kind of funny and sad and—"

"How do you ever have the guts to try out for things, anyway?" Nancy wanted to know. "I'd be scared stiff. You're never afraid of anything, Jody. So tell me about it. Did you get the part?"

Nancy and I had both been eight when her

family moved in up the street from our house, and we'd been best friends ever since. I was used to the way she chattered on and on, and I didn't usually get mad the way some people did when she wouldn't let me finish a sentence. She reminded me of a sparrow, chirping and hopping along, cocking her head and darting quick knowing glances this way and that.

I didn't really want to talk about the tryout, and with Nancy around I didn't have to. I coasted all the way home on her tireless stream of words. She filled me in on everything that had happened to her all day, and I didn't have time to think about my aching head until we said good-bye at her front walk.

Mark turned and grinned at me as Nancy disappeared. "Wow! She lost me somewhere back there between lunch and study hall," he said, and we both giggled. "Oh, hey, I meant to tell you. I signed up to work on the sets. So we'll be kind of together backstage, you know?"

"Great," I said, trying to believe that it really would happen. "I don't see how you'll have time, though, with basketball and everything."

"I'll make time," Mark promised.

Naturally when we got to my house Mark came in for a Coke. When we first started going together last spring my parents and my sister Kim and I always treated him like a guest. But by now it was as if he were part of the family. He knew where everything was and nobody fussed over him anymore.

On the way to the kitchen we said hi to Mom. She was cutting out curtains on the dining room table while Minnie, our tiger-striped cat, batted at a trailing corner of yellow fabric. Last September when Kim went away to college Mom and Dad had decided to redecorate her room. Of course Kim complained, asking why they had waited till she went away and why couldn't she be there to enjoy it. Anyway, when Mom wasn't at one of her classes or running around on errands for the American Association of University Women she spent her time poring over carpet samples and wallpaper patterns.

"Hi, Mark," she said, her mouth full of pins.

"Hi, Mrs. Chase. Hey, those are going to be neat-looking," Mark said, and he wasn't just trying to be courteous. He really looked at the rippling yards of cloth that covered the big round table.

"Thanks, Mark. Oh, Jody, you got a letter," Mom said. "From Mavis, I think."

I went to the letter rack in the front hall and recognized the thin airmail envelope and the British stamp. Mavis was my English pen pal. We'd been writing to each other since seventh grade and by now I felt like we really knew each other. It was hard to remember she was so far away we'd probably never meet.

Mark got a couple of Cokes for us and I tilted back in my chair at the kitchen table, reading about a rock concert Mavis had attended, and how her little brother had brought home a dead robin to dissect in the pantry. Mark leafed through an old copy of *Sports Illustrated*. Minnie sprang onto my knees. As I petted her I felt the pulsing rumble of her purr beneath my fingertips.

6

I noticed my sore throat more than ever as I sipped my Coke. My head thumped each time I moved. But as long as Mark was here I was determined to act as if nothing were wrong.

He stayed till almost six o'clock. We talked about how the school wanted to create a stricter dress code, and how the coach had suspended Bob Keller from the basketball team for smoking in the locker room. And I thought, gazing at his curly blond hair, his straight nose, and his sparkling blue eyes, how lucky I was to have found a boy like Mark van Huysen. He could have chosen almost any girl at school. Mark treated everyone with that extra bit of attention that made you feel he cared. But his really special smile was for me alone.

Really it was just an ordinary afternoon. It's funny how every detail is fixed in my memory. But when I look back on it now I feel like that day marked the end of a phase of my life—of the life I'd always taken for granted. As we sat over our Cokes at the kitchen table I didn't suspect that things for me would never be quite so smooth and simple again.

TWO

As I dressed for school the next morning my face stared back from the mirror flushed and hollow-cheeked. I felt a wave of dizziness as I stood brushing my long reddish-brown hair. But I had to go to school today. I had to find out about the tryout.

At the breakfast table Mom sized things up at a glance. She put her cool professional hand on my forehead and ordered me straight back to bed.

"Oh come on, Mom, I'm okay, I'm just —"

"Don't argue with your mother," Dad said, lowering the newspaper. "She knows what she's talking about."

Mom had been a nurse when she and Dad got married. She was taking refresher courses now and planning to get a job again soon, but she hadn't actually worked since Kim was born. I guess maybe she missed it. When she was plumping up pillows, bringing trays with soup and toast, and keeping track of doses of medicine she always seemed to be in her element.

8

Somehow today, as much as I hated to admit it, I knew that Mom was right. There was something irresistible about the thought of going back to bed.

"Oh, all right," I said. "I've just got to make one phone call." I glimpsed the quick look Mom and Dad flashed across the table — if I gave in this easily, they agreed without words, then I really must be sick.

Mark would have left already, but maybe I could still catch Nancy. She answered on the second ring. "You're staying out!" she cried. "You got the flu or what? A lot of people are coming down with it, you know — my aunt, and that kid down the street, what's-his-name with the —"

"Nancy, can you do something for me?" I asked. "Can you go to the bulletin board and just see if my name's on the list?"

"Sure. Then you want me to call you? Hey, I'll call you at lunch from the pay phone by the cafeteria."

"Tell her your mother says that's enough," Mom said loudly from the dining room doorway.

"I heard that," Nancy giggled. "I guess I get the message. Catch you later — get better, okay?" And that was probably the briefest conversation on record between Nancy Kowalski and Jody Chase.

As a former nurse, Mom was in her glory. My temperature was 102°, and when she called the doctor he phoned a prescription for penicillin to the drugstore on Wilmer Avenue. He agreed with Nancy; everybody was getting the flu lately.

Once I gave in to it I was amazed by how tired

I was. I must have fallen asleep the moment I crawled back into bed. Time dissolved into a long sequence of waking dreams when Mom made me swallow big capsules with tall glasses of water.

Sometime that evening Mom found me awake and told me that Mark was on the phone. "Nancy called a while ago, too, but you were asleep," she added. "She didn't leave any message, said she'd try later."

I sat up slowly and fumbled under the bed for my fluffy slippers. On my way down the hall I tried to clear the fog out of my head, tried to put time in order so I could sound bright and normal.

"I hope your mother didn't wake you up," Mark began. He hesitated, and suddenly I had the feeling that there was something he didn't quite know how to say. Then he burst out, "Listen, you ought to let me explain to Mrs. Ikeda. If she knew you were getting sick yesterday —"

"What do you mean?" I sat down heavily on the stool by the telephone table. I already knew the answer, but his words kept coming.

"Nancy called you, didn't she? About the play —"

"I guess she tried. Who got the part?"

"Some girl named Barbara something. Kalajian, I think. I don't even remember which one she was."

"I do. Dark brown hair, very thin. She read last, right after me. She was really good."

But Mark didn't want to hear it. He was all set to defend me. "Let me just talk to her," he pleaded. "Maybe she'll —"

"Don't, please. It was fair. I didn't read very well. I knew it even then."

"I thought you did fine. You should have gotten something, if not the lead then at least a smaller part."

"Mark, Mrs. Ikeda's really pretty fair. If I was the one she wanted, she would have given me a part."

But when I hung up at last and stumbled back to bed, disappointment lay like a weight on my chest. For months I'd dreamed of costumes and sets, of frantically memorized lines. I'd studied *The Barretts of Wimpole Street* until I'd felt I knew Elizabeth as well as I knew myself. But it hadn't been enough.

I was never accident prone, and I hardly ever got sick. I was usually healthy and full of energy — I liked to run even when I wasn't in a hurry to get somewhere. So how could this happen to me? How could I of all people lose out on being Elizabeth by getting the flu?

I was out of school for the rest of the week. Mom kept lamenting the good old days of Dr. Parsons who used to make house calls, but that must have been back before I was born. She and Dad agreed it would be silly for me to go out in the cold over to Dr. Ciccone's office, so I just stayed in and took my penicillin and little by little I started feeling better again.

I was undeniably recovered that Sunday afternoon when Mark dropped over. He said he was in the middle of painting one of his wooden dollhouses. Mark's father, who was from Holland, worked as a cabinetmaker. On the side he built dollhouses, and he had taught Mark to make them, too. They were wonderful, with real carpets, staircases, and windows, furnished with tiny, exquisite chairs and tables, bureaus and even lamps.

Anyway, Mark had been in the middle of working on one of his houses when he decided to drop over, and his pants were spattered with brown paint. I had the television on and I could hardly hear him over the noise of a Buick commercial. I caught something about his having to put on a second coat, so it sounded like he couldn't stay long.

"That's better," he sighed as I switched the set off. "Why do you turn it up so loud?"

"You sound like my mother. She's always complaining that I put the TV up too loud." I flopped into an armchair. "I've been so bored I can hardly stand it! You won't believe it — I've even been watching the afternoon soap operas. This morning I woke up wondering if Tom is going to leave Ruth for that blonde at the office."

"Wow," Mark said. "You've been hanging around here too long."

"I'll second that."

"Listen, I've been thinking." Mark paused long enough to whet my curiosity. "Maybe it'd be a good idea if you helped out with the play backstage, you know? Just to make Mrs. Ikeda remember you're alive before the next tryout."

For a moment, dragging around furniture and collecting props sounded like too much of a come-down after my dreams of being on stage. But then I remembered that spirit of working together that had caught us all up last year, that sense that every one of us was essential for the show to go on.

"What help do they need?" I asked.

"Oh, you know — costumes and make-up, sound effects, lights, and I think they still don't have a prompter."

"Hey," I said. "I wouldn't mind prompting." I would have to know the play backward and forward. I would feel that intimacy with the lines that was the magic of truly understanding a play, how it was put together, how the characters develop.

"Aha! Your practical, determined streak is surfacing," Mark said.

"It's just that I love plays," I said. "I'll be happy as long as I'm part of it. Hey, by the way, when do you have to finish your painting? Do you have time for a quick game of backgammon?"

We played one game before he had to go. But he left me with something to look forward to. There was a rehearsal tomorrow night, and I would be there no matter what happened.

I woke slowly, and in the first moments I didn't know what had dragged me back from my dreams. But the pain in my right ear was real enough. It throbbed and pounded as though my whole head was about to explode.

I turned my head from side to side but the

pain only followed me wherever I went. I wanted to yell like a little kid, "Mommy, I've got an earache!" But I didn't make a sound.

I curled into a tight ball under the blankets. I could just see the glowing dial of my alarm clock — two fifteen. Even if I woke up Mom and Dad they couldn't get hold of a doctor before morning.

Morning. I'd be all better by morning. This couldn't go on much longer.

I couldn't wriggle away from the pain in my ear but maybe I could get control of it somehow. A thought flickered through my mind, something I'd seen on TV once about self-hypnosis. If I concentrated, if I believed hard enough, I could make my earache go away. I could do it all myself.

I lay perfectly still and saw a deep hole before me in my mind's eye. It was as deep as a well — yes, there was even the mechanism for a bucket to be lowered and raised. And the pain would pour out of my ear and down, deep down that well forever.

Down ... away ... forever ...

Nothing happened.

Down the well, down to the bottom, I told the pain. *Go on, go away!*

I'd wait till three o'clock. If it wasn't any better by three I'd have to wake up Mom and Dad. Maybe they could take me to the emergency room.

But the pain would go away. Down that well, down to the very bottom ...

I pictured the pain like a fountain, leaping and churning and draining away. The more vividly I drew the picture in my mind the easier it was not to think about my earache. I began to feel like it wasn't quite so bad after all.

I must have dozed off finally, because the next time I looked at the clock it was four twenty-five, and in my ear lurked only the faint trembling echo of the pain that had become my whole world such a short time before. I pushed the memory of it down among my dreams and slipped gratefully back into sleep.

THREE

"There's no reason for you to be nervous," Mark said. We stepped out into the student parking lot and he slammed the car door. "What are you worried about, anyway?"

"Nothing, really." Of course Mark was right. It was ridiculous for me to feel so nervous tonight. But as I pushed open the door to the auditorium, already humming with people, I couldn't help remembering that I had been a miserable failure at the tryout for *The Barretts of Wimpole Street*.

Connie Friedman, the stage manager, dashed up to greet us. "Jody!" she exclaimed. "You're back! Wow! Good to see you alive and well." Connie's teeth were wired with braces, but that never stopped her from grinning.

"It's good to be back," I said fervently.

I spotted Barbara Kalajian as I draped my coat over an empty seat. She strutted across the stage, script in hand, reciting: "Oh, Doctor, I shudder to think what my life would be like if I hadn't a turn for scribbling and study . . ."

Barbara might have the lines down pat, but

Elizabeth Barrett wouldn't have been caught dead in those tight pants, I thought. But I was being catty. Barbara had won the part fairly and I had to give her a chance.

Mark gestured toward Mrs. Ikeda, who sat alone in the back row. "You might as well go talk to her now," he said, "before she gets started."

I glanced at my watch. At seven-thirty sharp the rehearsal would begin. I'd have five minutes to talk to Mrs. Ikeda if I began right now.

"Okay," I said. Mark gave me a little nudge and I started toward her up the long sloping aisle.

Mrs. Ikeda didn't look up until I was almost beside her. Then her face broke into a welcoming smile. "You're all recovered," she said. "Mark's been giving me progress reports, you know. He said you might be over here tonight."

Nothing in her look or her words said that I had slaughtered Elizabeth's lines. But I remembered. Glancing down at the script in her hand I glimpsed the names of characters I'd come to know so well — Elizabeth, Octavius, Arabel, Henrietta — and the old disappointment awakened somewhere in my chest.

Still I stumbled on. "Mark thought — I mean I — well we both thought maybe I could help out somehow."

Mrs. Ikeda regarded me coolly. "Well, let's see. I'm sure there are plenty of things Connie still needs—"

Sure, I thought. They'd always need someone to track down just the right pitcher to use as the tankard of porter in Act One. And they could always use an extra hand to drag Elizabeth's sofa out onto ths stage.

"Mark says you still need a prompter," I said in a rush. "I'd really love to prompt. I've already studied the play . . ."

"Oh, that'll be perfect," Mrs. Ikeda said. "I hadn't thought about it yet to tell the truth. I thought I'd just have to give the lines myself at first. But with you here to prompt I can concentrate on *how* they say things and not worry so much about *what* they say."

"You mean it's okay then? I—"

"Sit down," she said, suddenly businesslike. "We're blocking tonight, and they're supposed to know all of Act One."

She thrust a copy of the script into my hand and I took the seat beside her. It was seven-thirty, and the rehearsal was starting right on schedule.

Mark waved from the front of the auditorium and I grinned back, lifting my hand in a quick okay sign. 1 was part of the play now — I belonged to the team.

After the first ten minutes I had to admit to myself that Barbara really wasn't bad. They still hadn't gotten a sofa for her but she did her best to look like an invalid reclining on three metal folding chairs. Through most of the first act she hardly hesitated over her lines, and she had a lot to memorize, too. She was on stage the whole time while the other characters came and went. I began to wonder if I could have done as well myself.

The only problem was that Barbara spoke so

softly. Maybe she was just trying to get into character — Elizabeth was supposed to be frail and bedridden in the first act. Whatever her reason, I found myself leaning forward, straining to catch every word. I had the unsettling feeling that I might miss some crucial slip if my attention wandered for even an instant.

Every few minutes Mrs. Ikeda would stop everything to arrange and rearrange the positions of the people on stage. Octavius had to step closer to the windows, Septimus should lean against the mantelpiece, Henrietta should hover over Elizabeth. Was that why they called it blocking, I wondered — because the characters were moved around and set in place like building blocks to create the right effect?

Fred Margolis, who played Elizabeth's overbearing father, obviously hadn't spent much time learning his lines, and I had to help him out half a dozen times. He had a deep, rich voice that resounded through the auditorium, and it was easy to follow him. But Barbara! If only she'd speak up! And actually the girls playing Henrietta and Arabel weren't coming through very well either.

Just before the close of the first act, as Elizabeth was asking her maid to open the curtains, Mrs. Ikeda turned to me and asked, "Is it difficult to hear her, or is it just me?"

"I'm having a little trouble understanding her, too," I answered, relieved.

"She'll have to work on that," Mrs. Ikeda said, scribbling on her note pad. And when the act came to a close she launched into a lecture, the

19

first of the dozens I would hear between now and opening night.

"Octavius, Septimus, Alfred, all you brothers — I want your entrances fast, one right after another. You'll get good laughs if you keep the pace up. And you've all got to project — especially you, Elizabeth. I don't mean you've got to stand up there and yell. I mean throw your voice out to the whole auditorium. You should be able to whisper so that the whole audience can hear you. Just keep in mind that you're speaking to the deaf lady with the hearing aid sitting in the back row, and you'll be okay."

On the stage people shifted restlessly, and someone gave a nervous giggle. Fred Margolis said, "Hey, lady, can you hear me?" in a rasping stage whisper.

Mrs. Ikeda held up her hand for silence. "Let's go through the last part once more, and then we'll call it a night. Start right after Octavius' exit. Elizabeth says: 'Give it to me, please . . .'"

Barbara may have been doing her best to project, but I still couldn't hear her very clearly. When she suddenly stammered and came to a stumbling halt I had no idea what she had said last.

Panic-stricken, I searched down the page in my hand, but I had lost my place and none of the lines seemed quite right. What was the matter with me? I couldn't act and now I couldn't even prompt!

I glanced back at the stage, ready to grasp at any clue. Elizabeth's father had bent over her, grasping her hand — and suddenly everything fell back into place. As I looked at them I realized precisely where they must have gotten lost. "Oh, Papa, let us . . ." I called, trying to project in a stage whisper of my own. Barbara pounced on the line and finished, " . . . let us get this over and forget it. I can't forgive myself for having made the whole house miserable over a tankard of porter."

There was a lot more to prompting than I would ever have guessed. I'd have to follow along in my script, listen with all my might, and keep my eyes fastened on every gesture they made on stage.

But what about opening night? I thought with a start. I'd be prompting from backstage by then. I wouldn't be able to see a thing.

Well, it would work out somehow. By opening night Barbara and the others would have learned to project to the deaf lady in the back row.

After Elizabeth sobbed out the last moments of Act One again, I went backstage to find Mark. He and Connie were inspecting some sheets of plasterboard which would be used to create the set. But he scrambled to his feet when he saw me and asked, "Well, what do you think of the play so far?"

"It looks like it's coming along fine, if people just learn to speak up a little. Mostly everybody's doing well on lines."

Mark grinned. "We'll rig up a couple of hidden microphones on stage, how's that? Then they won't have to wear out their throats."

"Not a bad idea," I said. "You all ready to go?"

21

"Sure. See you, Connie."

Connie wished us both good night and we hurried out to the student parking lot. The temperature had dropped while we were inside and we ran to Mark's black Volkswagen bug, trying to keep warm. We slammed the doors and Mark flicked on the radio while the engine was warming up. Music flowed in around us, something soft and questioning by Paul Simon.

"So," Mark said, pulling out onto Wilmer Avenue, "how do you like prompting?"

"As a career?" I joked.

"No, just as a hobby. You're going on from here, you know. Really — you think you'll like it all right?"

"I'm so glad to be doing something," I said. "Especially after being stuck in the house last week. It's always exciting working on a play, on whatever level."

Mark took his hand off the steering wheel for a moment and closed it over my knee. "So you don't think you'll be bored, that's the main thing."

"I won't be bored," I promised. I listened to Paul Simon for a moment before I added, "If anything it's going to be a challenge."

FOUR

"They're all down in the rumpus room raising the usual rumpus," Nancy's mother told me when she opened the front door. She waved toward the door to the basement and I hurried downstairs, half an hour late for the January meeting of the Secret Society.

There was really nothing secret about it, and by now the old name was almost an embarrassment. It was a club Nancy and I had founded the summer before we started high school. We were terrified of leaving the secure, familiar world of elementary school and being thrust into the huge regional high school that served three whole towns. The club had been a way of keeping our old crowd of friends together. We'd begun with nearly twenty members, but year by year they had trickled away until now only half a dozen of us were left. But I still attended our monthly meetings faithfully, even though by now I had made other friends, had gotten caught up in Drama Club, and had discovered that Parkinson Regional High wasn't so overwhelming after all.

Nancy had a record blaring in the rumpus room. Connie and Louise were whacking a Ping-Pong ball back and forth. "Well, it's about time," Nancy cried, jumping up when she saw me. "Did someone tall, dark and handsome spirit you away or what?"

I stripped off my coat and dropped onto the vinyl-covered sofa. "Nothing so exciting. Try a history test I had to make up from when I was out sick."

"So can we get the meeting started?" Sylvia piped up from the far corner, where she sat ready with her note pad. She had appointed herself secretary, and for some reason, she was always determined to do everything by the books.

Nancy shrugged. "Why not? What else have we got to do?"

"Whoops!" exclaimed Connie, and she scrambled after the ball as it bounced over the bare cement floor. She got to her feet and laid the paddle and the ball on the Ping-Pong table. "I give up, I quit. You beat me again, Louise."

"Where's Mary Jo?" Sylvia demanded, as if some calamity would befall us if we lost another precious minute.

"Dolling herself up in the john, where else?" said Nancy. "Mary Jo Mitchell, will you get your body out here?"

"You don't have to shout!" shouted Mary Jo from behind the bathroom door. "Just wait a cotton-pickin' second, will you?"

"One . . . two . . . three . . ." Sylvia counted. Connie went over and flipped the record. She turned the volume up a little higher and came to sit next to me on the sofa.

"Jody," she asked, "what time is the —"

"Seven . . . eight . . ." Sylvia counted in her shrill voice.

"The what?" I asked Connie. "What time is the what?"

"Tomorrow, what time is —"

But I still missed Connie's last word. The bathroom door banged open and Mary Jo emerged, giggling, and still combing her frizzy brown hair. Sylvia applauded, and Nancy shouted something about wonders never ceasing; the record pounded on, and I clapped my hands over my ears and yelled, "Is it noisy enough for everybody around here?"

I don't know what they said to that because I kept my palms firmly in place over my ears until finally people began to settle down. I turned the record down low and at last the meeting began. I never did find out what Connie had been trying to ask me.

We all listened patiently as Sylvia read the minutes of our December meeting. We had spent most of it talking about holding a Christmas party, but for some reason it had never happened in the end. So as soon as the minutes were accepted as read (no additions or corrections), Nancy exclaimed, "Let's have a winter party. We can have it down here, my folks won't mind. And we can invite all the guys —"

"You've got to make it a motion," Sylvia interrupted her. "You've got to . . ."

"Sylvia, sometimes, I swear," groaned Louise.

Connie leaned over and whispered something to me, something about a book, but I couldn't make it out with all the racket. "What?" I demanded. "Which book?"

I could see Connie's lips moving, but only one or two words seemed to find their way out. One of them was "rules." I said, "You mean *Roberts' Rules of Order?*"

Connie nodded, but by then Nancy was on her feet declaring, "All right, all right. I make a motion that the Secret Society should hold a co-ed party."

We all burst into wild cheers and applause. Mary Jo's hand waved in the air and I guessed she was trying to second the motion, but even Sylvia would have admitted that was unnecessary.

"We've got to pick a day," Nancy said. "A Friday or a Saturday? How about —"

"A Saturday, a Saturday," Connie cried. "We'll have all day to get ready, and —"

"Wait a minute," Sylvia protested. "Nobody made a motion or anything. You can't just —"

The record stuck. Over and over it played: *Gonna be hap, gonna be hap, gonna be hap . . .*

"I don't believe this," I said. "Come on, can't everybody just talk one at a time? Nobody can hear what's going on."

Gonna be hap, gonna be hap . . .

Mary Jo jumped up with something about going to fix the darn record if no one else would.

But when she finally moved the needle ahead she also turned the volume up again. She looked over at me, grinning, and yelled, "That better, Jody?"

I glared at her and covered my ears again and at last she turned the music back down.

Connie poked me with her elbow. "If you don't like this much noise, what are you going to do when we have the party?"

"I didn't say I didn't like it. I just said — well look, we're trying to pick a date to have the party and how can we when nobody listens to anybody else?"

"Right on," called Sylvia. "That's why we need Parliamentary Procedure."

"How about Valentine's Day?" Louise asked. "I mean — I make a motion we have a Valentine's Day party."

"Forget it," I told her. "The Drama Club play's that weekend."

"Yeah, everybody's coming, right?" Mary Jo added. "I'm in it — I'm Wilson, the maid."

"Fred's in it, too, isn't he?" Louise asked. "We ought to get him to come to the party."

Mary Jo pounced on that one. "I didn't know you had a thing for Fred, Louise. Fred Margolis?"

"I didn't say I had a thing for him," Louise protested. "He's just fun at a party is all."

"You should see the way he acts at rehearsals," Mary Jo said. "He's always —"

"Well, what about the next weekend then?" Connie asked. "Why couldn't we —"

"— Jody can tell you," Mary Jo finished. By then I hadn't heard what I was supposed to tell.

27

Mary Jo watched me expectantly, waiting for me to bear her out. "What?" I said. "I didn't quite catch that."

"I was saying about Fred, at the rehearsals. The way he —" But again the words got lost somewhere between the pounding music and Sylvia's pleading, "Let's get back to the point!"

"I'm sorry," I said. I was starting to feel a little silly. "What did you say?"

Mary Jo flung up her hands in frustration. "I *said* he's getting so — oh just forget it, all right? What's the matter, are you deaf or something?"

"If I wasn't before I got here I probably will be when I go home," I said. "This is worse than the school cafeteria."

"Well, I can hear fine," Mary Jo said. "Maybe you ought to get your ears checked."

"Some people," I muttered. I'd never liked Mary Jo very much, ever since she told the teacher I had a Hershey bar hidden in my desk back in fifth grade. I probably wouldn't even see her anymore if she weren't a member of the Secret Society. She was always ready with some barbed remark, eager to laugh at someone else's expense.

But could Mary Jo be right? Was there really something wrong with my hearing?

Around me they were still discussing the party. But suddenly I couldn't think about it anymore. I remembered the trouble I'd been having at rehearsals, how hard I had to concentrate just to follow what people were saying on the stage. And at school sometimes I missed things that went on in class — but then, that happened to everybody, didn't it? Nobody could be expected to pay attention every second . . .

But I was paying attention here this afternoon. I was trying to listen to everybody, and still I kept missing bits of sentences here and there.

Well, I reminded myself, of course I couldn't hear, with everybody talking at once and the record player going and the noise echoing off the cement floor.

Only it didn't seem to bother anybody else . . .

"Jody, wake up," Nancy said, jarring my arm. "Can you bring them?"

"To the party? Sure, whatever you need."

"Cookies!" she said, exasperated. "Weren't you listening? I just said how you made the best chocolate chip cookies when you stayed over that time."

"I was thinking about something else," I said. This time it was true, wasn't it?

Nancy shook her head. "You're the only person I know who can come down with spring fever in the middle of January. Okay, Sylvia, put Jody down for cookies."

Now that everyone had calmed down a bit I could follow the whole discussion perfectly — the talk about refreshments and decorations, and of course the guest list. Everyone had something to say about that. But there was no doubt about whom I would invite. That was one of the nice things about having a steady boyfriend. I could always count on Mark any time I needed a date. It gave me a warm feeling to know he was out there, that we belonged together.

After a while the meeting broke up. Nancy

passed around pretzels and Cokes and Mary Jo turned the music up loud enough for her to hear it when she disappeared into the bathroom again to check on her make-up.

I didn't hang around very long; I had to get my homework done before rehearsal that night. Outside the street lights flickered, and now and then a car swept past me as I walked slowly along Jackson Road. I thought about Mark, who had a big math test he was worried about. I thought of the play, which was going better now that Fred had his lines down. By the time I reached home I had almost forgotten Mary Jo's words: *What's the matter, are you deaf or something?*

FIVE

"Save me, I am about to swoon," wailed Barbara, swaying toward a chair backstage. I couldn't help laughing. It was a perfect parody of Elizabeth in Act One.

"Beats me what I'm supposed to see in you, you old gimp," teased Dave Blackwell, who played Elizabeth's husband-to-be, the poet Robert Browning. "You better perk up or I might have second thoughts about all this."

I had to admit that Barbara had really mastered the part. Tonight, with her skillfully applied make-up, her eyes shone big and lustrous from her thin wan face. And act by act through the play she would gain color and life until in the end she and Robert Browning eloped and ran off to Italy.

Mark paused beside me, his arms loaded with a stack of books and a lamp he was carrying out to the stage. "How's it going?" he asked.

"Not bad," I said. "Are there many people out there yet?"

He nodded. "They're still selling tickets at the door, but it looks like it'll be a full house."

"Shsh! Here comes Mrs. Ikeda," Fred Margolis cautioned. Mrs. Ikeda had warned us countless times to be quiet backstage, as even the smallest sound had a way of floating out to the audience. We all fell silent now as she came into the dressing room. She looked regal in a long black dress and a string of pearls, her sleek dark hair coiled around her head and fastened in a knot at the back of her neck.

I expected her to deliver a last-minute pep talk, but instead she passed quietly among us, pausing to talk to each person for a moment before she moved on.

At last she stood in front of me. "Thanks, Jody, you're doing a great job," she said, smiling, and she slipped a small square envelope into my hand.

"What's this?" I asked, bewildered. But already she had turned away to say something to Connie.

I looked down at the envelope. It read only: To Jody Chase. But as I glanced around the room, I saw that she must be giving an envelope to everyone. Barbara was reading a note. Fred was showing something to Mark. The girls playing Arabel and Henrietta bent together, reading and whispering.

I tore my envelope open and drew out a folded sheet of note paper.

Dear Jody,

I'm so pleased that you have been part of this production. I have very much enjoyed working with you and I hope that your interest in the theater will continue and grow. We'll be putting on another show this spring, and I'd like very much to see you try out for a part. Thanks again for your help.

Sincerely,
Mrs. Gloria Ikeda

I read it again. The words seemed to dance off the page. Mrs. Ikeda hadn't given up on me after all. She still thought I could act, that I should try out for a part this spring.

She had written notes to each of us who had worked on the play. She had watched us carefully and had come to know us during the weeks of rehearsal, and she had something special to say to every one of us. And somehow I knew that for her we would put on a first-rate performance tonight.

Now they stepped out onto the stage to take their places. From where I sat I couldn't see them, but I knew that Elizabeth would be stretched out on her sofa, and her doctor would be standing beside her, ready to take her pulse. I pulled my folding chair as close as I could to the partition at the back of the stage. The murmur of the audience dropped as the house lights dimmed. "Curtain time," Mark whispered, hurrying past me. In another moment the curtains creaked open and I sat perfectly still, breathless with excitement to hear Dr. Chambers' familiar opening line: "Hmm — yes. It's this increasingly low vitality of yours that worries me . . ."

Their voices had a strange hollow ring from where I sat backstage, but I could hear each line distinctly. If anyone faltered I was ready to send out the critical words in a strong clear whisper.

I knew the play almost by heart, but now as I listened I imagined that I was out in the audience, hearing it all for the first time. I'd forgotten that so many of the lines were meant to be funny. But every now and then a ripple of laughter played through the audience, and the actors would pause for a moment as Mrs. Ikeda had instructed them, to let it crest and subside. I had never heard Barbara put so much emotion into Elizabeth's speeches before. This was going to be one of the best productions in the history of the Drama Club, and I tingled with pride, just knowing that I was part of it all.

Somewhere behind me erupted a flurry of whispers, but I tried not to listen. I wouldn't let my attention waver from the stage, not even for an instant.

"I put it right there on that table," said Connie in a low, tense voice. "It's got to be there."

"Well it's not there now," hissed Mary Jo. "Try to think, will you? She'll be out here to grab it in five minutes."

"Shsh! I'm trying to hear," I pleaded. But they paid no attention to me.

"I thought I saw it over there by those coats," Mark whispered. He darted past me and began tossing coats and scarves from a bench onto the floor.

From the stage I barely heard Elizabeth say: "No, Papa, that's really asking too much. I can't drink the horrible stuff in cold blood." This was the scene where Elizabeth's father insisted that she drink a tankard of porter, some sort of wine, I supposed. Elizabeth detested it, but her father swore that it had medicinal powers.

Then suddenly I understood. They'd lost the tankard! Elizabeth's tankard of porter.

"Why couldn't you just have one set place to put it?" Mary Jo asked Connie. "Then you wouldn't—"

"I can't help it if people go and move things!" Connie's voice rose and she sounded like she was fighting back tears. "I always put it right on that table, every rehearsal."

"Come on, keep it down, you guys," I begged again.

But they still scurried frantically back and forth, whispering, searching, lamenting. And time was running out . . .

I turned a page in my script. I hadn't been following closely enough, but the actors were still doing fine, oblivious to the commotion backstage. Well, they'd know about the trouble soon enough, when Henrietta dashed off for the tankard and returned empty-handed.

"Right here," announced Mark. He straightened up and lifted the familiar pewter pitcher high like a torch. Connie collapsed onto a chair, and Mary Jo muttered, "Well, just in time." I felt a surge of relief. The play would glide forward without a catch. Nothing would mar our perfect performance tonight.

From the stage came an ominous silence.

Now I was supposed to do something. This was my moment.

It was Henrietta's voice I'd heard last, but what had she been saying? Desperately I scanned the page before me, my heart thumping. Had she finished the lines where she argued to defend Elizabeth? Was it Henrietta who had forgotten a line, or should I be prompting Fred Margolis?

This couldn't be happening. But the slow painful seconds ticked away, the silence stretched thin. By now the audience must sense that something was wrong — and I was supposed to come to the rescue! If only I could have been watching the stage! It had been so much easier when I sat at the back of the auditorium.

"I have told you to get a tankard of porter from the kitchen!" thundered Elizabeth's father. I'd never heard Fred put so much force into those lines before. It was as though he had lifted everyone up and over a barricade in the road. Now at last they could roll along smoothly again.

It *had* been Henrietta who had gotten lost, then. Now it was glaringly clear. She'd blanked out on her line: "You're just torturing her because you like torturing." She had stood there, rifling through her memory, and I hadn't been able to help her.

"What happened? You lost your place?" Mary Jo wanted to know.

I glared over at her. "You didn't help any, making all that racket."

"I was going to help you and give her that line myself," Mary Jo went on. "The one about —"

"Shsh!" Mark stepped in front of her and came to stand beside me. "It's supposed to be quiet back here, remember?"

Reluctantly Mary Jo turned away. Mark added in a low voice, "Don't worry. It was only a second, and Fred filled in right away."

I should have been quicker," I said miserably. "It was my fault."

"It was our fault for making so much noise," Mark said. He patted my shoulder. "I bet they hardly noticed."

Inside my head I chanted the rhyme I'd made up back in fifth grade that day Mary Jo tattled about my Hershey bar: "Mary Jo, you've got B.O. Mary Jo, you've got B.O." It made me feel a little better back when I was ten, but tonight it didn't seem to help much.

I tried to concentrate on the play again, but nagging thoughts kept surfacing, demanding attention. What must Mrs. Ikeda think of me now? How could I hope to get a real part in a play when I couldn't even prompt without making mistakes? When the people in the audience noticed that long agonizing silence did they glance at their programs to see who was supposed to be prompting? Did they sigh and shake their heads when they read the name Jody Chase?

What was wrong with me anyway? Lately it seemed like my mind was wandering all the time

— but I felt as though I was concentrating as hard as I could.

I shouldn't have let myself be distracted. I'd started to worry about the tankard when I should have kept my thoughts focused on the play. But nothing was going to distract me again. The ceiling could fall in around me and I wouldn't flinch. My total being would remain riveted to the stage, and I wouldn't miss another syllable.

SIX

There were no more crises. No more props disappeared, no entrances were missed, and backstage everyone at least remained quiet, if not altogether calm. When Fred Margolis missed a line in Act Four, I whispered it so quickly that I hoped no one would have time to notice there was a problem.

So I was in high spirits when the curtains closed and the audience burst into wild applause, whistling and stamping. The actors all filed out to take their final bows, and Connie rushed past me with the big bouquet of carnations we had bought for Mrs. Ikeda. From where I sat backstage I couldn't see a thing, but the applause seemed to shake the floor. For a wistful moment I longed to be out there on the stage, bathed in triumph — but prompters don't go out for curtain calls.

But there would be another play this year, I reminded myself. Tryouts would be held sometime in March. And this time I'd be healthy and alert. This time I couldn't fail to get a real part.

Slowly the cheers and clapping subsided and everyone trooped backstage again. The tension that had held us in its grip all night had broken at last. Arabel and Henrietta collapsed in a fit of giggles. Connie and Mary Jo hugged each other. Everyone talked at once. "Congratulations!" I called to Barbara. "You were great!"

"I'm exhausted!" Barbara cried. "That last scene of mine is just so *draining*. I can't believe it's over."

"We did it!" Mark chortled. "I can't believe it — the set didn't fall apart, nobody tripped running out on stage, the lights didn't burn out . . ."

"You were all wonderful." Mrs. Ikeda stood in the doorway, holding her bouquet as though she didn't know quite where to put it. "I had the best time sitting there in the audience, knowing it was finally out of my hands. For the first time I could really relax and enjoy the play."

"Hey, everybody knows where my house is, right?" Barbara called. She had offered her basement for the cast party.

The thought of the party got us all moving. Mrs. Ikeda agreed to let everybody stay in costume, so most of the girls wore long Victorian dresses with billowing skirts, and most of the boys looked like they were dressed up to go to a funeral. But there was nothing funereal about the way we talked and laughed as we sifted through the coats and hats and scarves Mark had tossed onto the floor, telling each other again and again, with endless variations, the story of the lost tankard. Even Henrietta thought the whole thing was tremendously funny now that she realized I couldn't prompt her because of the commotion backstage.

Fred and Barbara and I all piled into Mark's car and drove over to Barbara's house. She lived in Morton, the next town over, in a big rambling ranch-style house on a hill. We went through the garage into the basement and I helped Barbara put out the food before the rest of the crowd arrived.

They came carload by carload. They came in stripping off coats and gloves, exclaiming what a cold night it was, and how delicious the hors d'oeuvres looked, and always, over and over again, how incredible it was to think that the play was really all over.

When Mrs. Ikeda arrived with her husband in tow, we all crowded around to get a look at him. I don't know why, but it's hard to realize that teachers have a life of their own outside school. So we were all dying for a glimpse into Mrs. Ikeda's secret life.

Mr. Ikeda smiled and nodded and shook hands with each of us in turn as fast as his wife could keep up with the introductions. He looked a little older than I had expected; there were streaks of gray at his temples and his forehead had the deep creases of serious thought. But he smiled brightly at me when my turn came up and said, "Hi, Jody. What did you think of tonight's performance?"

"I can't believe it's really over," I said, and we both laughed.

"I won't know what to do with all my new spare time," Mrs. Ikeda said. "Every afternoon I run home from school, grab something to eat, and run back for a rehearsal. I'll have to —" But the rest was drowned out by the record Connie put on. And over by the refreshment table Dave Blackwell, who had been Robert Browning forty-five minutes ago, began to recite a poem in a deep resonant voice — was it the beginning of *My Last Duchess*?

Whatever Mrs. Ikeda had been saying, it couldn't have been very important. I nodded as though I had understood and said, "I know what you mean. It's really been hectic, but I'm going to miss it."

Mr. Ikeda bent to say something close to his wife's ear. She said, "Sure, thanks," and he headed for the refreshment table.

Mrs. Ikeda turned back to me. "Listen, I hope you really will consider trying out for the show this spring," she said. "I've got some ideas —"

Just then Barbara's dog, a curly, little black poodle, scampered down the stairs to race around the room, yapping and leaping up on one guest after another. People greeted him with cries of surprise and delight, and somewhere what Mrs. Ikeda had been saying got lost.

"What about the spring play?" I asked her. "I'm sorry, I couldn't quite hear you with all the noise in here."

"Oh, don't I know it," she sighed. "I really wanted to come and be with you all tonight after the show, but I knew the noise was going to get to me."

"I'm glad I'm not the only one," I said. "But anyway, about the play —"

"Yes." Mrs. Ikeda leaned closer. "It's up to the Selection Committee to decide, of course, but there's one I'd like to do very much. Are you familiar with Ibsen's *A Doll's House?*"

"Oh, yes!" I exclaimed. "I read it last summer. I really loved it — he had such modern ideas about women for somebody writing back in those days."

Mr. Ikeda returned and handed her a cup of punch. "You ought to go over and see those hors d'oeuvres, Gloria," he told her. "This girl's family must have been in the kitchen all day."

"Oh, yum! I think I will," Mrs. Ikeda said. "Anyway, Jody, keep it in mind." She waved her hand and wandered away to the refreshment table. I looked around for Mark.

He stood with Barbara, Fred, Mary Jo, and a crowd of others over at the far end of the room. Directly above his head hung the stuffed antlered head of a deer, probably a trophy Barbara's father had brought home from some hunting trip. I hurried over.

"They really should have," Barbara was saying. "I don't know why we couldn't —"

The black French poodle burst into a new frenzy of yapping. Someone was dragging in a bunch of clattering metal chairs. I was being buried in an avalanche of noise.

"Couldn't what?" I asked. I wondered if any of them would be able to hear me.

Mary Jo did. "What? What? Which? Who?" she mimicked.

"The show!" Barbara raised her voice to be heard over the din. "Why couldn't they let us do

43

the show two nights instead of just one? Just on account of midterms, they said, but that's dumb — they've never said that before."

We all agreed. Now that the play was over we were ready to do it all again from start to finish.

Mary Jo pointed at "Robert Browning" who was still trying to command an audience over by the refreshment table. "One thing about Dave," she said, "he sure needed Barbara."

"Oh, he wasn't too bad really," I said. "I mean, Barbara was terrific, but Dave managed okay on his own."

Mary Jo gave me a puzzled look. "Who said anything about Barbara? I said Dave sure needed a *barber!* You don't think Robert Browning wore his hair like that, do you?"

I felt my face flush hot. "I know," I said quickly. "I kept thinking Mrs. Ikeda would tell him he had to get a haircut."

"You thought I said he needed a Barbara!" Mary Jo giggled. "You really ought to get your ears tested. A *Barbara!*"

I had reached my limit. I had had enough of Mary Jo. "There's nothing wrong with my ears!" I exclaimed. "I'd be able to hear fine if somebody'd just turn down that damn record!"

They all looked at me in amazement. No one spoke. Even the poodle stopped its yapping. For one long moment the whole room hung suspended in a quivering, unnatural silence.

It was Mark who broke the spell. "Jody," he said in a strange, tense voice, "the record ended five minutes ago."

SEVEN

I guess Mark was surprised that I wanted to leave early, while the party was still in full swing. But he accepted my excuse that I was tired. We said our polite good nights to Barbara and thanked her for a lovely time.

It was a relief to be away from the tumult of Barbara's basement. Now the low hum of the motor was the only sound. Little by little I began to relax, to feel normal and whole again.

"That was kind of a weird party, don't you think?" Mark said as we turned onto Jackson Road.

I leaped at the chance to justify leaving early. "I'll say. When Fred put that hat and glasses on the deer's head I just thought, 'Oh, no, I've got to get out of here.'"

But that wasn't quite in character for me, I thought. At any other party I would have laughed along with everyone else.

Mark stopped in front of my house and shut off the motor. But he didn't move to open the door. "You know," he said, "with the play and everything, I bet you forgot what day it is."

I stared at him, bewildered, as he reached into his pocket and drew out a small, square box adorned with a red ribbon. Then suddenly it came to me. "It's Valentine's Day!" I cried. "You're right, I did forget. I forgot completely."

"I didn't." He grinned and pressed the box into my out-stretched hand.

Inside, carefully wrapped in tissue paper, was a tiny, heart-shaped, wooden box. "You made this," I breathed, turning it carefully in my hand. I'd seen dozens of Mark's miniature chairs and tables and cupboards, but this little box was special. It was so simple, and yet so perfect.

"Well, open it," Mark urged. My fingers felt clumsy as I lifted the tiny lid. Inside, nestled on a bed of cotton, lay a silver pin. It too had the shape of a heart.

"Wow!" I said. "It's so delicate — it's beautiful." Then I turned to Mark and kissed him. "Thank you," I said. "What a Valentine's present."

"You really like it?" He could tell that I did but he still wanted to hear me say it.

"I love it," I told him. "The pin is lovely — but the box — how can you make something so small?"

"Oh, it wasn't so hard. I just sort of worked on and off for a while."

"Sure," I said. "You make it sound so easy."

Mark looked at me closely. "You're cheering up, that's the main thing. You look a lot happier now."

He was right. By now I'd almost forgotten how desolate I'd felt when we had left the party. Mark really cared for me. As long as I had him nothing could go very wrong in my life.

But suppose . . . No, it was too horrible to imagine! Still — suppose I was beginning to go deaf? Would Mark still want me then?

I looked away as he sat there smiling at me, his hand folded over mine. The thought that I could lose him hurt too much. "I guess I better go in," I said. "My mother'll be waiting up."

"Oh, all right," Mark sighed. We stepped out into the bracing cold and he walked me to the front porch. "Parting is such sweet sorrow," he said as we stood together under the porch light.

"That I shall say good night till it be morrow," I finished. We'd said those lines to each other a hundred times before.

But how many more times would we say them now?

"Hi," Mom called over the clamor of the TV as I shut the front door behind me. "You're back early, aren't you?"

"Not really." I stuffed my coat into the hall closet and glanced at my watch. "It's quarter to twelve. The party was starting to break up."

"How was the play? Everything go all right?"

I went to stand in the living room doorway. Mom had set up a card table in front of the television, and there she sat, sifting through a litter of papers and envelopes, absorbed in some new project. Every few moments she glanced over at ths television to keep tabs on Humphrey Bogart as he swaggered across the screen. Dad was away in Cincinnati on one of his business trips, and we both missed him. Mom handled that by becoming even busier than usual.

"It was a good show," I told her. "You should have come. The place was packed."

"I thought about it," Mom said. "I half made up my mind to go and then Marge Clark called and said that Dot Henshel was supposed to do this mailing for the AAUW, but one of her kids has a broken collarbone, and it all has to go out Monday morning so —" She waved her hand helplessly over the table.

"You could have said no," I pointed out.

"If I haven't learned to say no by now I guess it's a lost cause," she laughed. "It's a good thing your father's not here. I was just saying the other day I wasn't going to get involved in one more thing. He'd never let me live this down." She moistened the flap of an envelope with a damp sponge, pressed it closed, and asked again, "So the play went off all right?"

"Fine," I said. But somehow I didn't want to talk about it. The thought of the performance only reminded me how I'd failed to prompt Henrietta. And when I remembered the cast party I could only picture a jumble of noise and lost pieces of conversation.

"Hey, Mom," I said, eager to change the subject. "Mark gave me a Valentine's present. It's beautiful — look!"

Mom leaned forward and I handed her the box. "Oh, that's marvelous!" she exclaimed. "How does he make these things? I can understand building big things like bookcases, but how can he make something so tiny?"

"I don't know. But he can make just about anything."

"Mark's a pretty terrific guy," Mom said, handing back the box and the pin. "You'd better appreciate him."

"I do," I said fervently. "I know, he could have any girl at school he wants. So why should he pick me? I can't figure it out."

I was startled to hear my own words. I'd never wondered before why Mark should be interested in me. And I'd never doubted that I could keep him interested, either. But tonight everything felt suddenly shaky.

"Well, I think Mark has good taste," Mom said staunchly. "Don't worry about — oh, he's going to say it!"

She held up her hand for silence and we both turned to the screen just in time for Bogart to utter his immortal line: "Of all the gin joints in all the towns in all the world, she had to walk into this one."

Just as well that I hadn't had time to say anything else about Mark and me, I thought. No telling what I'd have blurted out. I needed to get off by myself and sort everything out. "Well," I said, after we watched a few more minutes of *Casablanca*, "I guess I'll go up to bed. I'm beat."

"Good night," Mom said. "See you in the morning."

"Good night." Slowly I climbed the carpeted stairs. As I rose toward the empty upstairs hall my worries seemed to press more and more tightly around me. But it was ridiculous to let them take over like this, I told myself. There was nothing the matter with my hearing, nothing at all . . .

I shut my door, blotting out the steady murmur from the television downstairs. I kicked off my shoes and sat on the edge of the bed, wrapped in silence. It was quiet enough to hear a pin drop, Mom might have said — but of course you couldn't in here, not with the carpet.

Still I ought to be able to hear especially well now, with no voices or music or yapping dogs to distract me. I would prove to myself here and now that my ears were perfectly all right.

I slipped my watch from my wrist and, holding my breath, raised it to my right ear, eager for the reassurance of its steady rapid ticking.

But there was no sound. Nothing. Only the fierce ringing silence.

My hand began to tremble.

My watch must have stopped. I gave it a brisk shake and listened again. But still the ticking hadn't started up. I stared at the face behind the crystal. Five past twelve. So twenty minutes must have passed since I came home — yes, that seemed about right . . .

My heart was pounding as I lifted the watch again, to my left ear this time. Was it only my imagination — no, this time I knew I heard something even above the strange drumming inside my head — there was an unmistakeable patter, just the delicate hint of a sound. But it wasn't enough to fill me with relief. It was too thin and fragile, just the echo of what I thought the ticking of a watch used to sound like.

Panic rose in my chest. I snatched a little bell from my bureau and shook it sharply, first by my left ear, then beside my right. My left ear reported a soft tinkling, but my right ear caught only the faintest quiver of a sound that should have rung bright and clear.

I had to get control of myself, I thought desperately. If I could just keep calm . . . But I clapped my hands, I slammed the drawer of the bureau, I opened a book and snapped it shut, straining after sounds whose existence I had never questioned before. Tonight, in my panic, they all seemed thinner, more remote than they once had been.

I had to be imagining all of this. If I could just calm down and think it out I'd see that it was mind over matter. I was worried about my hearing, so naturally my ears didn't seem to be working properly tonight.

But when had I started to miss bits of conversations? When had the ticking of a watch and the ringing of a bell made their retreat?

Maybe I'd always had a little trouble hearing what people said when there was a lot of noise around me. It was hard to remember for sure. But I'd begun to notice the problem especially when I went back to school after I was out with the flu.

And a thought jolted me like an electric shock. That earache! Had it all begun with that terrible earache? That awful twisting pain seemed so far away now but I knew it had tormented me once. I had lain awake willing it away.

And it had gone at last, and I had fallen asleep. But had something of that night stayed behind?

I huddled on the edge of my bed, my head in my hands, my stomach in knots. I didn't want to believe it. This couldn't be happening to me. Not to me, Jody Chase! I was hardly ever even sick, I was at the top of my class, I'd always had plenty of friends and I went out with Mark van Huysen. There couldn't be something wrong with me!

But the truth hammered at my brain, relentless, inescapable. I was losing my hearing. Maybe I was going to be deaf.

I had to tell Mom. I'd race downstairs, fling myself into her arms, and through my sobs I'd plead for her to do something. She was a nurse — and besides, she was my mother. She'd have to know how to help me.

Barefoot I went out into the hall. But at the top of the stairs I paused. The television still murmured. Mom would still be sitting at her card table, stuffing and sealing all those envelopes. What exactly should I say to her? "Mom, there's something the matter with my ears. I can't hear very well anymore." No, I'd have to slide into it slowly: "Mom, I've got to tell you something. See, I've got this awful problem —"

But even if I could get the words out, what could Mom do? She would take me to a doctor, and he'd confirm what I already knew. Maybe he'd say I had to wear a hearing aid. They might even stick me in a special school for deaf kids where I'd learn to read lips and make strange signs with my hands.

I turned and tiptoed back to my room. I closed the door and sank onto my bed. What had I done to deserve this? It wasn't fair. I was only sixteen and suddenly my whole life was falling apart.

I could just picture Mary Jo gleefully telling everyone that she had guessed it all along. None of the girls would know quite what to say to me. They'd feel sorry for me and try to be nice, but I wouldn't be one of them anymore.

And how would Mark feel when he found out that I wasn't really normal? Boys want girls to be pretty and fun to have around. They didn't want you if you were a miserable bundle of freakish problems. Sure, Mark would try not to hurt my feelings. But why would he want a girl who was practically deaf?

It was the thought of Mark that brought the tears at last. I lay on my bed in a shuddering heap, my face buried in my pillow, and gave in to the sobs that had been fighting to take control over me.

Somehow I finally got undressed and burrowed under the covers. I must have dozed off, because I woke to hear Mom come into my room and turn out the light. She was right there with me, but still I was utterly alone.

Then the house was still. Its silence crept up around me and at last I fell into a fitful sleep.

* * *

My sleep was full of restless, disjointed dreams, but they faded away as I woke. There was nothing left of them but the first lines of a poem my grandmother had taught me when I was very little: *Birdie with a yellow bill, Sat upon my window sill* . . .

Sunshine streamed in through the curtains. From the kitchen wafted the fragrance of frying bacon. Mom made pancakes and bacon for breakfast every Sunday without fail.

Then I remembered everything — my confusion at the party, my silent watch, my despair as I cried myself to sleep.

But in the soft light of morning nothing could really be hopeless. Now, as I dressed, my mind began to deliver clear, rational messages to me. My life hadn't collapsed yet. Maybe I couldn't hear perfectly but I certainly wasn't deaf. And I hadn't lost Mark yet, either.

Mark always teased me about my determined, practical streak. I thought of that now as I stood before the mirror brushing my hair. It was silly to let my imagination run wild. No one really suspected how bad my hearing was. Even last night people had been ready to laugh it off, to assume that I daydreamed a lot, that I couldn't stand noise, maybe that I was just a little bit peculiar. Mary Jo was always cracking jokes, and Nancy teased me about getting spring fever in January. But they still didn't take my problem seriously. The fact was that I was getting by all right.

There must be books about hearing and the things that could go wrong with it. Tomorrow afternoon I'd go to the school library and see if I could find any information. Probably my ears weren't half as bad as I had thought last night.

Until I knew for sure there was no point saying anything to Mom or anyone else. Maybe there was something wrong with me, and then again maybe it was nothing at all. In either case, for the time being I would keep it to myself.

From its little heart-shaped box I took Mark's silver pin and fastened it to the collar of my blouse. Then I ran downstairs to breakfast in stockinged feet.

EIGHT

It was easy enough to get rid of Nancy that
Monday afternoon. She was waiting by my
locker, hoping we could walk home together, but
she sighed in sympathy when I told her I had to
spend this afternoon down in the school library.
I'd been so involved with the play, I said, that I
hadn't even started my History paper, and it was
due in a week.

And Mark had a basketball practice today. He
would assume I'd gone straight home, and
wouldn't even look for me when he got finished.
The whole afternoon was mine, and it couldn't
have been easier.

The library was hushed and almost empty — a
perfect place for me, I thought, as I draped my
coat over the back of a chair. The librarian
glanced at me as I made my way to the card
catalog, and I nodded a terse greeting. I glanced
stealthily around the room to be sure no one was
watching me. Then slowly, almost fearfully, I
pulled out the D drawer to look for books on
deafness.

Eventually I selected half a dozen books from the shelves and piled them on a table in the back. From where I sat, facing the door, I'd be able to spot anybody who might come in. If someone approached me I could cover up the books and pull out an innocent notebook in time.

It was almost exciting, this game of intrigue I had begun to play. I might be the mysterious romantic heroine of some play, my life built around a dark secret . . .

But there was nothing romantic about the stack of books on the table before me. I regarded them with dread. Whatever they were ready to tell me I didn't want to know. Yet at the same time I felt compelled to open them and look for answers to the questions that tormented me. What was wrong with my hearing? Was it going to get worse?

Cautiously I opened the first book and flipped through the pages. It contained the biographies of twelve deaf men and women. From what I read I found out that they all had been to school, they had jobs and families — but suddenly I snapped the book shut and shoved it aside. Why should I read about people like them? They were deaf. They lived in a world without voices or slamming doors or radios, a world that had nothing to do with mine. I didn't hear very well, but I certainly wasn't deaf.

There was a book about American Sign Language, and one about the education of deaf children. One after another I pushed them aside. None of these books had anything to do with me.

The last book looked almost like a medical text, and I wondered what it was doing in our high school library. Slowly I leafed past the pages of acknowledgments and the long, uninspiring introduction. I wouldn't find anything here. I could go home and put worries out of my mind. My ears weren't that bad anyway. I was getting by . . .

I turned one more page and there, glaring up at me, was a color cross-section of the human ear. It was all there, the eardrum and those three little bones behind it, the coiled chamber of the inner ear that they called the cochlea. I studied it, fascinated, wondering. Somewhere in this diagram the key to my problem lay buried. If something was wrong with my hearing I was looking at it right here on page 26.

I returned the other books to the shelf and settled down for a long session with *Hearing and Hearing Impairments*. It was heavy going. The book was dense with terms like "auditory dysfunction" and "conductive disorders." It referred to the tympanic membrane, the stapes, and the organ of Corti as though everyone knew what they were.

I was almost ready to admit defeat when I spotted the heading, *Symptoms of Hearing Loss*. Beneath it was a list of twenty warning signs. Apparently it was a questionnaire for ear doctors (they were called otologists, I had discovered) to give to their patients.

This was it. This simple list of questions would tell me if I was just imagining my problems or if I really suffered from a hearing impairment.

The room felt suddenly very hot. My hands were sweating. Maybe I should just close the book and pretend I had never found that list of questions.

But I had come to the library to get some answers. I couldn't go home empty-handed.

I began at the top. *"Do you try to avoid situations where there is a high level of noise?"* Yes. *"Are you ever accused by your friends and family of hearing only what you want to hear?"* Well, maybe . . . *"Do you usually hear men much better than you hear women?"* Yes.

Slowly I worked my way down the list. *"Do you often ask people to repeat their last names when you first meet them?"* Well, I guess so. *"Do you usually want the TV or radio to play louder than other people in your family do?"* Yes.

When I got to the end of the questionnaire I tallied up my answers. I had given *yes* responses to twelve of the twenty questions. To three more I had answered *maybe*. According to the explanation on the next page my answers indicated that I had a "mild to moderate" hearing impairment.

I closed the book and sat gazing into space. It was true. I'd known it even before I came down to the library, but now I could no longer even pretend to myself. I could be a case from the pages of the book that lay on the table in front of me. I was one of the hearing impaired.

My life lay before me, a parade of special classes, special devices, special treatment. Once people found out that I wasn't normal they'd

never let me forget it. I could sit home alone at
night, watching the captioned news on TV . . .

The only deaf person I'd ever known was my
Great-Aunt Dora. She lived in Denver so we
didn't see her very often. She wore a hearing aid
but you still had to speak up to talk to her. She
seemed to understand Dad pretty well, but Kim
and I always had to shout, and even then she
wasn't too clear on what we were saying. Com-
municating with her was such a strain, I always
looked for excuses to be somewhere else when
she was around.

Would people start to avoid me because it was
just too much trouble to make me understand
things?

At the front of the room the librarian rose and
went to the closet for her coat. "I'm closing now,"
she called to me. "Do you want to check that
book out?"

I hesitated. I ought to read everything I could,
find out exactly what I would be facing. I could
tuck the book among my other books so no one
would see the title. I could read it in my room
tonight, carefully and thoroughly, without the
fear that I might glance up to find someone peering curiously over my shoulder.

I opened the book again and rippled through
the pages. I should study those diagrams and
charts. I should try to understand what they
meant by decibel levels . . .

Then, from the middle of a paragraph, a line
seemed to spring out at me. It grabbed my attention and compelled me to read the paragraph
straight through. "Influenza and other respiratory

diseases can cause infection of the middle ear resulting in hearing loss ranging in degree from mild to very severe. Fortunately, however, such impairments can often be alleviated, given prompt medical intervention."

Prompt medical intervention. The words blazed up from the page, accusing and undeniable. Then my hearing probably *was* damaged by that attack of flu. And maybe it could have been saved, with *prompt medical intervention.*

"Didn't you hear me?" said the librarian sharply. "I asked you if you want to take that book out."

"I heard you fine," I said. "No, I don't think so." I'd already read enough, more than I wanted to know.

I put the book back in place on the shelf. I dragged on my heavy winter coat and double checked to be sure I had all the books I needed for tonight's assignments. As I stepped out into the corridor my mind raced back over the weeks. More than six had slipped by since the night I woke up with that earache. If only I had told Mom and Dad about it the next morning. I could have gone to Dr. Ciccone, just so he could check me over. But no, I hadn't wanted to miss another day of school. I was going crazy hanging around at home. Besides, I was determined to go to the rehearsal that night. But what did one day of school and a rehearsal matter, compared to my hearing?

Maybe there was still hope. I'd tell Mom as soon as I got home, and she'd make me a doctor's appointment right away.

But what good could that do now? Six weeks had already passed. Nothing they did now could be considered prompt medical intervention.

I paused by the main office to button my coat and pull on my gloves. Anyone who passed me would see a slender girl of medium height with reddish-brown hair (I'd always liked to call it auburn), wearing boots and a gray wool coat. She would be carrying an armload of books — just an ordinary high school junior starting home on a Monday afternoon. No one could tell by looking at that girl that she was different from everyone else around her, that she was handicapped.

By not telling Mom and Dad about my earache I had brought all this on myself. I would blame myself for the rest of my life. But I couldn't endure having Mom and Dad, and the doctor, and Nancy, and Mary Jo, and Mark ask me again and again, "Why didn't you say something? Why on earth did you wait till it was too late?"

I had reached the foyer when steps pounded behind me and Mark's unmistakeable voice called, "Hey, Jody! Jody, wait up!"

At any other time I would have been delighted to run into Mark unexpectedly. I would have dashed to meet him, full of news, eager for all the talk and laughter and affection we always shared.

But today I felt a surge of dismay. I'd thought I would miss Mark completely. How could I face him this afternoon? I needed to be alone, to think. But with Mark I would have to be bright and cheerful, as though nothing were wrong.

I turned and waved to him as he strode toward me. I put on my best smile and called to him. "Hi! I thought you'd still be at practice."

Mark shook his head. "It's five o'clock. How come you're still here?"

"History," I said with a groan. "You know, that stupid paper." I might as well keep the story straight, I thought. You never could tell when Mark and Nancy might compare notes.

"How's it going?" Mark asked. "You get much done?"

"Not as much as I should have," I said truthfully. "How was practice?"

"Just fair. Davidson's getting over-confident. He's going to blow that Brookvale game. Oh, hey, by the way, which night is that party again? The one with your club, your Secret Society?"

The party! How had I forgotten about the party? I'd invited Mark three weeks ago, but I couldn't go now. I couldn't struggle through a whole evening in a noisy crowd like that, I couldn't . . .

"Oh, that party," I said, stalling for time. I'd tell him it had been called off. But then he was bound to hear about it from somebody else . . . "Why do you ask?"

Mark looked at me in surprise. "Well, because I was planning to go with you, but I forgot which night it is, and then this afternoon I realized we've got the Brookvale game Friday night and I was afraid it might conflict."

"No, the party's Saturday." If I had any acting talent at all, why couldn't I keep that dull hopeless note out of my voice? "It doesn't conflict with the game — only — only I don't know if I can go."

We stood just inside the double front doors. Mark stared at me and I gazed miserably down at my boots. "Why not?" Mark demanded. "What's the matter?"

I fought down my rising panic. Mark had to have an answer. He deserved an answer right now. But I couldn't think fast enough. I had planned my trip to the library so neatly this afternoon — how could I have forgotten about that wretched party?

"Well, I've got that paper," I faltered. "I hardly got started even, and —"

"Your paper!" Mark exclaimed. "Oh, come on! You'd never miss a party on account of a dumb History paper."

"Well, there's always a first time." I tried to laugh it all off. "You know, I read the other day that people learn more slowly as they get older. It seems like that's true for me — ever since I turned sixteen I'm working harder and accomplishing less."

"Jody." Mark looked at me hard for a long second and didn't say anything else, just, "Jody."

I longed to burst out through the front door and run, all the way home, to leave Mark far behind me shouting his questions to the wind. But I couldn't. I had to talk my way out of this somehow.

"I just can't go, that's all," I told him. "I'm really sorry, but I just can't."

"Okay, okay." Mark shoved the door open and we stepped out into the biting cold. "I just wish you'd tell me what's going on, that's all."

"What do you mean?" I flashed. "What makes you think something's going on? I told you, I've got this paper for History —"

"It wasn't that History paper that made you want to leave the cast party the other night. Just level with me, that's all I'm asking you to do."

If only I could! If only I could pour it all out to him. "I've got that paper," I said doggedly. "That paper and — just a lot of things to do."

"All right, if you say so," Mark said, and lapsed into silence. I pulled up the hood of my coat to stave off the wind.

"You should have driven today," I said, vainly hoping we could find our way back to ordinary details. "We're going to freeze walking home."

Maybe Mark's answer was only a grunt. Whatever it was it came through vague and far away, muffled by my hood. Cold as it was I tossed the hood back again and walked on, past the parking lots and the playing field, out to Wilmer Avenue.

"Look how overcast it's getting," I tried again. "They said it might snow tonight. Hey, maybe we'll have a blizzard and they'll call off school tomorrow."

"I doubt it," Mark said, thrusting his hands into his pockets. "Listen, Jody, I don't know how to ask you this exactly — did I do something or say something that's bugging you? Are you mad at me for some reason?"

"Oh, Mark!" I cried. "Of course not. How could you even think that? We can go to the party," I added desperately. "If you really want to we'll go, it's okay with me."

Mark shook his head. "Come on, what do I care about the party? It's just that I don't know what's happening with you lately. But if something's bothering you, I sure wish you'd tell me what it is."

I could tell him right now how I didn't dare go to the party because I'd make a fool of myself again asking what people said to me. I'd tell him about the horrible things I'd read in that book this afternoon, and how scared I was, and how awful it felt to know that there was something wrong with me. Mark was an understanding person. Maybe I really could tell him. After all, Robert Browning had loved Elizabeth Barrett even when she couldn't walk.

But that was only in a romantic play. I remembered how Dave Blackwell had teased Barbara backstage: "Beats me what I'm supposed to see in you, you old gimp!" That was the way people reacted in the real world.

Mark might be understanding about most things, but if he knew I couldn't hear it would probably ruin everything. No boy would want to go out with a girl who was hearing impaired.

"Nothing's bothering me," I said lightly. "Why should I want to keep anything from you?"

"I don't know," Mark said. "But if you ever tried it wouldn't be all that easy."

He took his right hand from his pocket and reached out for my hand. Even through my glove I got a good, warm feeling. Maybe some-how nothing would ever have to change between us.

But Mark already suspected something. And it was true, it wouldn't be easy to keep a secret from him. He knew me so well that sometimes I felt as though he could read my mind.

I would have to put my acting ability to the test. Somehow I would find a way to act like a girl with perfectly normal hearing. And no one would ever have to know the truth about me. Not Mom or Dad, not Nancy or Mary Jo, not Mark. Never Mark.

NINE

"And then Sylvia said she wouldn't be caught dead up on those uneven parallel bars," Nancy chattered. "You know how stubborn she can get — she just sat there and wouldn't budge, not for anything."

"I can just picture it," I said. I opened my locker and put on my coat. Carefully I sorted through my books and decided I didn't need to take home Algebra or American Lit.

"So then Old Lady Muller comes up," Nancy went on. "And you know how she talks, kind of through her nose, right? So she says, 'Now, girls, everyone in my P.E. class has to take a turn, without exception.'"

She paused for a moment as I giggled appreciatively. Together we started down the hall toward Stairway J. Locker doors banged and two boys shouted at each other, something about a set of car keys. I didn't quite catch what Nancy said next, but with her that never made much difference. She just chattered on and on, never really expecting an answer.

If only it could be as easy everywhere else. In Lit class this morning a big truck had been idling outside the window and a couple of people behind me were whispering and giggling about something just as Miss Laurier called on me. I hadn't heard the question, I couldn't even fake it. I just stumbled around like an idiot saying, "Umm — umm," until Miss Laurier gave me a funny look and asked me if I was getting enough sleep lately.

Our footsteps echoed in the stairwell. A flight below us somebody switched on a transistor radio and the crackle of static and a fractured song billowed up to us. "So finally there she was swinging up there," Nancy was saying, "and you should have seen the look on her face. Not exactly scared, you know, but indignant, like, 'How dare you require this of me!'"

We were both laughing as we emerged into the first floor corridor. I could just imagine Sylvia swinging from the parallel bars, ungraceful and indignant, despising every moment of it. "How did she get down?" I asked, hoping there was still more to the story.

"Old Lady Muller started freaking out," Nancy giggled. "She thought she was going to let go and just fall on her head or something. So she goes rushing over there, shoving everybody out of the way, and she's going, 'Don't panic! It's all right! I'm right here with you!'"

"That must have been the clincher," I said. "Who wouldn't panic with Muller hovering around?"

We stopped by the main office and Nancy put

on her red woolen scarf, tossing the fringed ends over her shoulder. She studied the bulletin board while I put on my gloves and rearranged my armload of books. "Hey, look at this," she exclaimed. "You ought to enter, Jody."

I followed her pointing finger. There among the patchwork of notices about the Hi-Y dance and the International Club's trip to the U.N. was a small oblong slip of paper which read: "One hundred dollar first prize offered for the winning essay on 'How Handicapped Workers in My Community Are Proving That Ability Counts.'"

"You write real well," Nancy was saying. "Just think of all the things you could do with a hundred dollars."

All I could picture was a row of men and women standing at an assembly line, their hands moving like well-oiled machines, their faces as empty as their lives. They were all deaf, oblivious to the roaring noise around them. I might escape for a moment into Nancy's stories, but they were out there somewhere waiting for me, ready to claim me as one of their own.

"Sounds depressing," I said, turning away with a shudder.

"What?" Nancy demanded. "A hundred dollars? What's so depressing about that?"

"No, not the money," I said, exasperated. "The essay."

"Yeah, well, maybe." Nancy shrugged. "Still, it'd be worth it, don't you think?"

"No, I don't."

I guess I said it a little too vehemently. Nancy gave me one of her funny sparrow looks, cocking her head on one side. "Well, whatever you say," she said. "If I could write I'd try it. Hey, you going to that basketball game tonight?"

"I don't know," I said. "I missed the last one, so I promised Mark I'd try to go this time." But when I thought of how the gym would rock with stamping and shouting, the way I wouldn't be able to hear a word if someone tried to speak to me, I wondered if it was a promise I dared to keep.

"That team from Long River doesn't stand a chance," Nancy said. "They've only won two games this season. It's going to be a boring game, but I guess I'll go. It's better than hanging around home watching the tube."

She chatted on as we crossed the foyer and stepped outside into a cold, steady drizzle. I pulled my hood up over my head; with Nancy it hardly mattered if I lost a word here and there. Lately she was about the only person I could really relax with. It was so simple to drift along on her stream of talk. When she paused I'd just nod or giggle or ask what happened next? and she'd launch straight into another story.

If only I could feel so safe with Mark. These days I felt like he was always studying me, waiting for some slip that would give me away. With Mark I had to be quick and alert, straining to catch every word. Sometimes it was exhausting trying to smile and laugh with him, pretending I had heard things I could only guess at.

Lunch in the cafeteria was the worst part of my day. Mark and I had eaten lunch together nearly every day this year. But now I felt submerged by the babble of voices and the clatter of trays. This week I had told him I had a lot of studying to do. Day after day I'd barricaded myself behind a pile of books at a table crowded with strangers. And I was careful to arrange myself so Mark would have no room to pull up a chair and join me.

But I missed him so much! If only I could show him somehow that I still cared for him as much as ever.

That was why I really had to go to that game tonight. Maybe it would be so noisy that no one else would be able to hear either. I could go with Nancy. Probably Connie and Mary Jo would turn up, too. We could sit right down in front where Mark could see me and I'd clap for him until my hands were sore.

I jumped aside as a car swished through a puddle, spattering my legs with mud. "It was Mary Jo that started it," Nancy was saying. "She thought it was kind of funny, and she said something to Louise, and then — you know how that stuff goes around."

I hadn't even been trying to listen, and obviously I'd missed something. Probably it was nothing very important. If I paid close attention now maybe I could piece the story together.

"Oh, Mary Jo's always starting things," I said lightly. "Nobody takes her too seriously."

Nancy gave a vigorous nod. "I wouldn't even mention it to you if it was just Mary Jo. With her you're better off ignoring whatever she says. But these past couple of days a lot of other people have been saying things, too. And I figured since we've been friends such a long time —" She hesitated. "I figured if you had to hear it from somebody you were better off hearing it from me."

Hearing what? What had Mary Jo been spreading around school?

Suddenly my hands went cold inside my gloves. My knees felt loose and unsteady. Mary Jo had guessed. She had told everyone. The school was buzzing with it. And all this time I'd thought I was guarding my secret so well.

"What are they saying?" I asked in a small, tight voice.

"I don't exactly know how to put it," Nancy said. "I mean, don't get me wrong. I keep telling them they're crazy. It's just that you've been acting kind of weird lately — not going to that party and eating by yourself — so people have been wondering . . ."

"What are they saying?" I repeated. My knees were really shaking now. I wondered if Nancy noticed. But I had to know, I had to hear it all.

Nancy took a deep breath. She opened her mouth and closed it again. Then suddenly her words exploded into the rainy afternoon. "They're saying you must be pregnant."

I stopped in the middle of the sidewalk and gaped at her. It must be another trick of my ears — I couldn't have heard her right. "What?" I demanded, flinging my hood back onto my shoulders. "They're saying what?"

"I said I didn't believe it myself." Nancy was red to the roots of her hair. "You know how people love to make things up."

"They said I — they're really saying I'm pregnant?"

"Look, I'm sorry." She turned away miserably. "I shouldn't have said anything. I never know when to keep my big mouth shut."

For an instant I almost laughed with relief. My secret was still safe. They hadn't guessed, they weren't even close.

But in the next moment the meaning of Nancy's words crashed in upon me. I was just another petty rumor, the subject of cafeteria gossip. "Mary Jo, you've got B.O.," I muttered.

It was Nancy's turn to say, "What?"

"Nothing," I said. It didn't help today. It hadn't helped in years.

Mark would hear this, if he hadn't heard it already. How could I face him? How could I go back to school and face any of them again?

"Don't worry, Nance." As though from across a great distance I heard my own voice saying the lines that had to come next. "It's not your fault. Like you said, I was bound to hear it sooner or later."

Nancy looked over at me almost timidly. "But there is something bothering you, isn't there? You have been — different lately."

"I'm perfectly all right." How many times had I said those words already? How many more times would I repeat them, that same hollow old refrain nobody seemed to believe?

For once even Nancy had run short on things to say, and we walked on up the hill in a strange silence. At her front walk she asked, "You want to come by tonight? We can walk over to the game together."

How could I sit there with our old crowd and cheer whenever Mark made a basket? How could I act as though I'd never heard their stories? All the time they laughed and joked with me they were thinking and guessing, and when I was gone they whispered their thoughts and guesses behind my back.

How would Mark feel about all of this? Would he be as embarrassed as I was, or would it be easier for him to laugh it off? What could I say to him? Should I bring it up myself, or should I just hope against hope that he wouldn't hear it at all?

"I'm not sure I'm going," I said slowly. "I'll call you later and let you know, okay?"

Nancy frowned. "Hey, you're not mad or anything, are you, Jody?"

"No, don't be silly. It's just — well, really I've got a ton of homework tonight."

I'm all right. . . I've got homework . . .

The cold rain spattered against my hair and trickled down my forehead into my eyes. Slowly I walked the last block home, alone.

TEN

It just wasn't working. All my efforts to protect my secret had gotten twisted and tangled — and now they said I must be pregnant. I could kill Mary Jo! It was just the sort of rumor she loved to spread. How many times had I heard her talking about other people — how Laura Lugano got caught shoplifting, how Sue Bartlett's big sister was planning to elope. I never had dreamed that one day Mary Jo would be telling her stories about me.

Well, people were bound to wonder, to talk. They could see that I had changed. I avoided people, I sat and brooded by myself. I wasn't convincing anyone that I was perfectly all right. I was trying to act like a girl with normal hearing, but my performance was falling apart.

I unlocked the front door and threw my coat and books onto a chair in the den. The noise of a radio drifted down from Kim's room. Mom must be up there doing some redecorating.

Slowly I climbed the stairs. As I approached Kim's room the noise evolved into music, one of those classical programs that were on in the afternoons.

I would tell Mom everything. I could no longer bear the feeling that nobody on earth understood what was happening to me. Sure, Mom would demand to know why I hadn't said anything before. I didn't know how I would answer her. But maybe there was still time. Maybe if I went to a doctor right away he'd say it still wasn't too late to do something.

Anyway, I was making a mess of things by myself. I couldn't drag this secret around with me forever. I had to tell someone.

I stood in the doorway before I heard the rasp of Mom's scraper above the strains of Beethoven. Inch by inch she was laying bare the original plaster of Kim's walls. Here and there the old wallpaper still clung in ragged patches, or hung in long trailing tatters, its faded flower pattern reduced to meaningless splotches of blue and yellow and red. Wearing a spattered white apron, her hair tied back out of the way, Mom stood on a stepladder, her hands encased in thin rubber gloves.

"Hi, Mom," I said.

"Oh, hi. I didn't think it was time for you to be home already." She peered down at me in surprise.

"It's quarter to four," I said. How should I begin? I couldn't just say, *Mom, I'm a little bit deaf*, could I?

"Quarter to four!" Mom exclaimed. "I've been at this since one-thirty and —" She turned away to survey her work just as the orchestra struck a crescendo, and I didn't hear what she said next. But she looked back at me as though she expected an answer.

This was my perfect opportunity. I could simply explain, *Mom, I really didn't hear you. See, I've had this problem lately —*

But the words wouldn't come out. "What did you say?" I asked. "I didn't hear you with the music and all."

"Oh, it was nothing important. Go ahead, turn that thing down." Mom jumped down from the stepladder and stripped off her gloves. "I need a break. I think I'll put on some tea — want some?"

"No, but I'll have a Coke."

This would be much better, I thought, as I followed Mom downstairs into the kitchen. I couldn't hope to have an important talk while she was perched up there scraping around near the ceiling. But sitting quietly at the kitchen table I could pour out the story from the very beginning, from the night I woke up with that terrible earache.

Mom bustled around putting on the kettle, and I got myself a glass and a chilled can of Coke. It gave me a peculiar feeling, sitting down with Mom this way. I might be a character in one of those TV family programs, preparing for the heart-to-heart talk that would set everything straight.

Usually Mom and I were both so busy we just

tossed greetings and questions at each other and dashed off, hardly waiting for the answers. Now she poured her tea and I sipped my Coke and we looked at each other as though neither of us quite knew what to say.

My heart started to throb. I had to plunge in now, right now, or I'd lose my nerve. "Mom," I said, lowering my class. "I — I kind of want to talk to you about something."

"Sure." She stirred in a spoonful of sugar. "What's going on?"

I hesitated, groping for words. "Well, it's hard to explain. It seems like — like I've got this problem." I came to a full stop. *I can't hear,* I wanted to shout. *Maybe I'm going deaf.* But the words would be so condemning, so final. They refused to come out.

"With Mark?" Mom asked helpfully.

"Well, not exactly." I thought of the way Mark would react when he learned the truth about me and amended, "Well, I guess it is, in a way."

"Are you two having some kind of disagreement?" Mom asked. She paused before she added, "You know, come to think of it, you haven't brought him around much lately. I thought he was just busy with basketball. It never occurred to me —"

"No, that's not it," I assured her quickly. "He is busy with practices just about every afternoon. The thing is, I —"

The telephone let out a long, insistent ring. "Oh, no," Mom sighed. Neither of us moved. The phone rang again.

"You better get it," I told her. "It's probably for you."

"Peace, peace, but there is no peace," Mom chanted, but she threw me an apologetic glance and went to lift the receiver. "Hello?"

This was only a temporary reprieve, I reminded myself. I'd still have to tell the whole story the minute she hung up. But maybe this would be an especially long conversation. Maybe somehow I was being spared.

"No," Mom said in exasperation. "No, Mildred Zeller was supposed to . . . Oh, for heaven's sake."

I swirled the ice cubes in my glass. Maybe my hearing really wasn't all that bad. Right now I could understand everything Mom was saying. I could hear her voice perfectly. Maybe it wasn't worth getting her all worried over nothing.

She'd really make a fuss, too, if she thought there was something the matter with me. All her nursing instincts would have a chance to run wild. I wouldn't be able to stand it. Besides, suppose the doctor said it was really too late to do anything about my hearing now. If I'd gone a couple of weeks ago it would have been different, but now he could do nothing. That would be the worst of all.

"Listen, I really can't," Mom was saying. "Honestly, I could do it tomorrow, but if it's absolutely got to be this afternoon —"

I had to laugh to myself. No matter what she promised herself Mom could never turn away anybody who pleaded hard enough.

And she was giving in again. "How much stuff

is there? . . . I'll be able to carry it all myself? . . . No, you're right, it's not far, and we can't afford to miss out on it . . . I will, okay. I'll get back to you. Bye."

Mom turned back to me, flinging up her hands in despair. "I never learn, do I? Now I'm supposed to jump in the car and run over to Morton for a big load of clothing — the clothing drive for the children's hospital, you know? These people are going to throw everything out if nobody collects it this afternoon."

"You remind me of that song from *Oklahoma*," I said, and sang, " 'I'm just a girl who can't say no . . .' "

Mom glanced distractedly around the room and her gaze lighted on her half-filled cup. She picked it up and poured the last of the tea down the sink. "Oh, Jody," she said. "You were right in the middle of telling me something. About you and Mark?"

In another minute she'd be pulling on her coat, racing off on her errand. The timing was all off now. Just as well, anyway. "Oh, it wasn't really important. Just, you know that Mary Jo Mitchell? She's been going around spreading all kinds of nasty rumors about me, and I was thinking what will Mark say when he hears it? What makes people do things like that anyway?"

"Is that what's bothering you?" Mom said. "Just ignore her. I don't know why you hang around with that girl anyway."

"I won't after today," I told her as she left.

I didn't follow her to the front hall, but I knew

she would be tugging a comb through her hair, rummaging for her car keys, grabbing her coat out of the closet. "I won't be long," she called. "Your father's got an office meeting, we'll be eating late. Are you going out tonight?"

"I'm not sure," I said, but the front door closed and my words dangled in the sudden silence.

I stood alone in the kitchen, feeling the emptiness of the house close in around me.

I went up to my room and sat down wearily on the edge of the bed. I had taken the coward's way out. But how long could I go on like this? I was afraid to speak to anyone about my fears, but I couldn't endure the loneliness of my secret. If I could just tell one person, maybe it wouldn't seem quite so overwhelming. But no one I knew could listen without thinking of me in a different way.

Suddenly an idea seized me. There was someone I could tell, someone far away who didn't know my family or any of my friends.

I went to my desk and took a sheet of flowered note paper from the middle drawer. For a few moments I sat motionless, gnawing the end of my pen. Then, at last, I began to write:

Dear Mavis,

I really enjoyed your last letter, especially the part about your trip to London. Mavis, I've got an awful problem and I haven't been able to talk about it to anyone. For the past few weeks I've been noticing more and more that there's something wrong with my hearing . . .

Once I started writing I couldn't seem to stop. I filled page after page with the trouble I'd had prompting, the lines I'd read in that medical textbook, the rumor Mary Jo was spreading, and the question that haunted me — what would Mark do if he ever found out? I felt lighter and freer as the pages piled up on the desk before me. "I guess this is what people mean when they say you need to unburden yourself," I wrote. "I feel better already, just telling you about all this. Maybe I'm just imagining half the trouble anyway. I don't think my hearing is really all that bad. I'll be able to get by if I just don't let it get me down."

I didn't realize how much time had passed until the phone rang. I felt renewed, ready for the world again, as I sprinted to the landing.

I lifted the receiver and put it to my left ear; lately the voice on the other end sounded clearer that way. "Hello?" I said. I waited for some female voice to inquire, "Is your mother home? When will she be back?"

But instead it was Mark's voice on the other end. "Hi," he said. "How's everything?"

Had he heard yet? Should I bring it up myself? I couldn't — I'd die of embarrassment!

"Hi, Mark," I said, my heart fluttering. "I'm okay. How was practice?"

"Not bad. You're coming to the game tonight, aren't you?"

My throat went dry. "I really wanted to, only — I —"

"You heard then," Mark said quietly. "I

thought you would have. Somebody told you what those idiots are saying."

"It was Nancy. She told me on the way home today." Then my words tumbled out in a rush. "Mark, I don't know how I can face them — they'll all be staring at me and whispering . . ."

"It's disgusting!" Mark said fervently. "It makes me so mad I could—oh, never mind. But listen, Jody, you can't hide. You've got to stand up to them. Just act like everything is perfectly fine."

I'd been trying to do that all along. If I'd been more successful Mary Jo's rumor could never have gotten a foothold. "I know," I said. "But how can I?"

"Don't pay any attention to them," Mark said. "Come to the game tonight, have a good time, and don't even think of what anybody might say. That way you'll show them you've got nothing to be ashamed of, right?"

Of course he was right. And if Mark wanted me to go to the game tonight I'd go. "Okay," I promised. "I'll go — for you."

"Great. I knew you would. Only Jody —" Mark hesitated. "There *is* something wrong, isn't there?"

For an instant the words sprang to my lips. It had been so easy to write it all to Mavis. Maybe it wouldn't be so hard to tell Mark after all. He'd been so understanding about this gossip at school . . . But this problem with my hearing was different. Could I expect a boy to be understanding about that, even a boy like Mark?

Just act like everything is perfectly fine.

"I've just been in a funny mood lately," I assured Mark. "Don't worry, I'm snapping out of it."

"Okay," Mark said doubtfully, "if that's all it is. I'll see you at the game. And afterward, you want to go out for a pizza?"

"Sure, let's." I winced at the thought of the blaring jukebox. But I'd go. I'd smile and laugh as though everything were perfectly fine. I'd do whatever I had to not to lose Mark.

ELEVEN

Nancy and Connie and I sat together at the game that night, and we yelled ourselves hoarse. With all the noise in the gym, nobody tried to converse. I had a glorious time, cheering and clapping harder than anyone else every time Mark made a basket.

We beat Long River easily, just as Nancy had predicted. In the excitement of victory I piled into Mark's car with Connie and Nancy and Ted Davidson from the basketball team, and we drove over to Joe's Pizza. Packed into a booth, the jukebox pounding, I could hardly follow the conversation. But somehow it didn't seem to matter much. I laughed when the others laughed, and listened quietly as they rehashed the game.

"I'm glad you convinced me to come tonight," I said to Mark later, as he drove me home. "Maybe my being there will help stop some of those rumors. Anyway, I had a good time. I'm sorry I've been acting so weird lately."

Mark hesitated as though once again he was about to ask me what had been on my mind. But to my relief he seemed to think better of it. "I'm glad you came, too," he said. "I was starting to miss you."

"Me, too," I said awkwardly. "Thanks for being so patient with me."

"Oh, I don't know that I've been all that patient," Mark said. "Hey, let's sit together at lunch tomorrow, okay?"

Lunch . . . in that noisy cafeteria . . . But the cafeteria couldn't be much worse than a booth at Joe's Pizza, could it? Maybe I'd learned something tonight. When the others laughed I'd laugh too, even if I hadn't heard the joke. And if I wasn't sure what was going on I'd just keep quiet. That way I wouldn't risk making ridiculous mistakes, and I wouldn't be saying "What?" all the time, either.

"Sure," I told Mark. "I'll see you tomorrow at lunch."

But despite my brave intentions my heart sank as Mark waved me to a crowded table the next day. I longed to retreat with my books back to my solitary corner, safe from a medley of unintelligible questions, free from bursts of laughter that had no source I could understand.

Well, I told myself, I would just have to act. It was time for me to get into character and make my entrance. I smiled a greeting and maneuvered my laden tray through the crowd to the place Mark had saved for me beside him.

Barbara, the former Elizabeth Barrett, said hi from across the table. Beside her Fred Margolis glanced up and smiled at me. And Nancy slid over a seat so she could sit next to me. With Mark on one side and Nancy on the other, I told myself, I ought to feel secure.

Naturally Nancy was doing most of the talking. Even against the babble of voices and the clatter of trays from the tables around us I could follow most of her story. At assembly this morning she had discovered that the boy in front of her had brought an old cow-bell which he plotted to ring in the middle of the principal's address. She put down her fork and gestured with her hands to show how he had carried it, tucked out of sight under his stack of books.

Then Fred Margolis guffawed and exclaimed, "Oh, yeah, I know who that guy is. Hank something. He pulled a stunt like that in study hall last week."

Suddenly everyone was talking at once. I missed the end of Nancy's story and never knew if Hank something had rung the bell or not. I caught something Barbara said about waking the dead, but that still didn't tell me what had happened.

"That'll be the day, right, Jody?" Mark said, grinning.

"That's for sure," I agreed, returning his smile. I dug into my spaghetti and hoped no one would ask me anything more demanding than that.

"Hank goes with the weirdest-looking girl, she looks like Dumbo," Fred said. "Her ears stick out like this." He held his hands beside his head and flapped them back and forth.

Suddenly I wasn't hungry anymore. My spaghetti seemed doughy and tasteless. That was how boys talked if they could spot the least little thing the matter with you. You were a hopeless freak if you were too fat or had too many freckles, or if your ears stuck out a little . . . So what would they say about a girl like me who could hardly even hear?

I glanced sideways at Mark to see how he had reacted. He wasn't laughing, but that probably didn't mean much.

And while I was still thinking about boys and how they judged people, the conversation was getting away from me again. Barbara turned to Fred and said something that sounded like "Tickle us." *Tickle us?* What could she be talking about? I searched through my mind, trying every combination I could think of: *pickle us, jiggle us* . . . But nothing fit.

Watching their faces, straining my ears to catch everything they said, I pretended to be intent on my salad. "Oh, no," Nancy giggled. "I don't believe it." She turned to me expectantly and I gave her what I hoped was a knowing smile.

Tickle us . . . *Ridiculous!* That was it! I should have figured it out in the beginning. But what were they talking about?

Suddenly Nancy picked up her purse and scraped back her chair. She said something to me but most of it got lost behind a burst of raucous laughter from ths next table. She looked toward the lunch line and then back at me as though she expected a reply.

She was going back to get something else to eat, that was pretty clear. Then she must have asked me if I wanted her to bring me something.

"Sure, thanks," I said. "Get me a piece of that white cake — it looked pretty good." I fished in my wallet and handed her a couple of quarters.

"At your service," Nancy said, returning to the line.

I had done it right. I was starting to learn. And if I could hold my own in the cafeteria I could manage anything.

"Jody," Barbara said suddenly, leaning toward me. "Are you trying out for *A Doll's House?*"

"The tryout!" I exclaimed, nearly dropping my fork. "Already? I didn't think it was so soon."

A couple of girls two tables away broke into a rollicking rendition of "Happy Birthday." I didn't catch everything Barbara said, something about the play being in May and there being hardly enough time to get ready. But when she said, "The tryout is next Monday after school," her words came through strong and clear.

"I guess you're trying out," I said, striving to keep my voice level.

"Well, of course," Barbara said. "Nora's a fantastic part. I'd love to get it."

I thought of Nora Helmer. It would be a wonderful challenge to portray the changes in her character. When the play opened she was giddy and childlike, pretending that she didn't have a thought in her head because that was how her husband wanted her to be. And by the close of the final act she became an independent woman, setting out on her own.

Well, I might be able to handle lunch in the cafeteria with the old crowd, but how could I face a tryout, rehearsals, a performance where there was no room for mistakes?

"I'd really like to try out," I said slowly. "But, well, I guess I just haven't got the time."

"Why not?" Mark demanded. "I thought you were planning on it. And Mrs. Ikeda said herself —"

"I know," I said. "I thought about it some. But I really better not."

"Too much homework to do?" Mark asked ironically.

What did he mean by that? Was he saying that he didn't believe me, that he suspected that something more serious lay beneath my excuses? I threw a wild glance around the room, searching for some way to change the subject before it got beyond my control.

And Nancy was coming to the rescue. She headed straight for our table, a dish in each hand, and surely her arrival would create just the distraction I needed.

But Nancy's arrival was going to be a mixed blessing. Right behind her trotted a girl with frizzy brown hair. Mary Jo Mitchell.

"One cake." Nancy set the dish before me and dropped two nickels change beside it.

"Hi, guys," Mary Jo said, pulling up a chair. "I already ate. I just thought I'd come join you people when I ran into Nancy."

After the things she'd been saying about me how could she look me in the face? But she could, and she did. "Hey, Jody," she said. "I haven't seen you around much lately. How are you feeling?"

What did she mean by that? Was she probing for some hint about my "delicate condition"? "Oh, I'm fine," I said brightly. "How about you?"

Mary Jo shrugged. "Who knows, after lunch in this cafeteria."

But Barbara refused to be distracted. "Mrs. Ikeda's got the scripts," she told me, picking up where we had left off. "I went and got one this morning."

"You mean for that Drama Club play?" Nancy broke in. "You're going to try out, aren't you, Jody?"

"Well, I don't know." Almost instinctively I turned to Mark for help. But he only looked back at me, bewildered.

"You're not going to try out for *A Doll's House*?" Mary Jo demanded. Her eyes sparkled with eagerness. I could just picture her whispering across the aisle before her next class: *She's not even trying out for the play! Bet I know why . . .*

"I said I don't know," I told her. "Maybe."

Suppose I missed a cue? What if I couldn't hear the directions Mrs. Ikeda gave from the back of the auditorium?

Barbara half-turned and said something to Fred Margolis. For an instant he hesitated. Then he nodded and said, "I wasn't planning on it, but I probably will. I can't resist."

I hadn't heard her question clearly, but I was certain Barbara had asked Fred if he had intended to try out. This was like solving a problem in algebra, deducing the question by knowing the answer. And I was learning to balance these strange new equations.

Acting in a play might be easier than talking to people in real life. At least in a play I would know in advance what people were about to say.

Maybe it wasn't so farfetched after all. If I watched every gesture and concentrated on every word, why couldn't I try out for a part in the play?

Besides, if I tried out for *A Doll's House* I would prove to everyone that I really was perfectly all right. If I got a part and acted it without a hitch, Mary Jo and the others could put aside their doubts about me forever.

"I know just what you mean," I told Fred. "I keep thinking how plays take up so much of your time — but still I can't resist." And I looked straight at Mary Jo as I added, "I probably will end up trying out. I guess I don't have much choice, do I?"

Mark beamed at me and I grinned back. *No, I haven't changed,* I wanted to tell him. *I'm still the same as ever.*

"I knew you'd do it," he exclaimed. "And this time you won't be coming down with the flu, either. Maybe you'll get the lead part."

I thought I saw Barbara wince. If she only knew that this time I'd have to battle something a lot worse than a sore throat and a headache. "There are a couple of other girls' parts," I said hastily. "I don't have to try out for Nora."

93

But suddenly, for the first time in a long while, an old longing stirred within me. I wanted to study lines, to practice movements and expressions before the mirror. I wanted to plunge in and work with the team until our performance was filed smooth and flawless. And even though I was "hearing impaired" I might still have a chance.

At least, I thought, *I was going to find out.*

TWELVE

Once I read somewhere that if you're anxious about an appointment you tend to arrive ahead of schedule. I guess that proves how nervous I was about the tryout for *A Doll's House*. When I entered the auditorium that Monday afternoon, script in hand, the place was totally empty.

I took a seat toward the front and read through some of Nora's speeches again. She changed so much as the play went on that it would be almost like learning to portray two or three characters instead of only one. Still I felt as though I understood Nora. She had built her life around a secret. Years before, in desperate need, she had secretly borrowed a large sum of money. I knew how she felt as the action unfolded, acting as though everything was perfectly fine while, unknown to the people around her, the moneylender hounded her with threats and warnings.

I ought to understand Nora, I thought. I'd been practicing her part for weeks now, every day, in my own life.

More people began to wander in, scattering themselves through the room. Some talked in little clusters, low-voiced and tense. Others sat alone like me, poring over scripts and silently mouthing lines. The atmosphere reminded me of the frantic moments before the start of a final exam.

Mrs. Ikeda breezed in at three-fifteen, and immediately the tryout got underway. She cast the boys' parts first, probably because it would be relatively easy. So few boys were trying out that, as usual, there wasn't much choice. It looked like Fred Margolis would be Torvald Helmer, Nora's husband. It was the same sort of pompous, domineering role he had played as Elizabeth Barrett's father, so he ought to be in good form. And a boy named Art Mavrovic seemed ideal as the vengeful despairing moneylender, Krogstad.

The last of the boys had just finished reading when Barbara Kalajian sauntered in. She settled into a seat at the end of the row where I was sitting and placed her script on the empty seat beside her. If my early arrival proved that I was anxious, did Barbara's late arrival mean that she was casual and relaxed about the tryout? She looked almost bored as she watched the proceedings, but maybe it was all an act. For an instant I wondered if she was intentionally trying to make me more nervous than ever.

No, probably Barbara wasn't even thinking about me. But everything put me on edge this afternoon. I couldn't help remembering that afternoon back in January when I stood on the stage, stumbling over the lines I had studied so hard. And today could be far worse. Would I be able to hear when Mrs. Ikeda told me where to begin?

"Okay, how many want to try out for Nora's part?" Mrs. Ikeda asked. I raised my hand to join the forest of waving arms that sprang up. There were really only five or six but to me just then there seemed to be dozens.

"Well, let's get started," Mrs. Ikeda said. She pointed to a girl in the front row. "What's your name?"

I didn't catch what the girl said, but neither did Mrs. Ikeda, because she said, "I'm sorry, you'll have to speak up a little."

"Kathy Ferone," the girl said more clearly. It was nice to know I wasn't the only person who made people repeat things. Maybe this tryout wouldn't be so awful after all. If only Mark would come. He knew I was trying out today and he had promised to come by and give me his moral support. Somehow I was sure I'd feel more confident if Mark was sitting here beside me.

Kathy Ferone didn't read badly, I concluded, but I knew I could do a better job. I felt even more reassured by the two or three girls who followed her. They read flatly, as though they didn't understand what their lines were about. Probably they'd never even read the play straight through. They wouldn't be much competition. But there was still Barbara, suppressing a yawn at the end of the row.

Mark hurried down the aisle and slipped in to sit down by me just as Mrs. Ikeda sent Barbara up to read. "Sorry I took so long," he said in a low voice. "I got hung up talking to Mr. Lopez about my science project. I've got to see him before school tomorrow, too. Did you go up yet?"

I shook my head. "Not yet," I said. There was no time to say more — Barbara stood on the stage, thumbing through her script to the page Mrs. Ikeda had asked for. I sat motionless, straining to catch every word and intonation, searching her face for every flicker of expression.

Barbara was good. In the opening scene she was buoyant as a lark. But when Mrs. Ikeda had her skip ahead into Act Two she became taut and fearful. And when she read from Nora's final speeches at the close of the play, she was calm and resolute. My spirits sank. I wondered if I could ever do as well, even if my hearing were perfect.

Mark seemed to guess my mood. He touched my hand and bent toward me to whisper something, but I didn't catch his words.

"What?" I whispered, turning to face him.

He whispered again, but I still didn't understand him. Flustered, I asked "What?" again. I leaned closer, struggling to grasp his words. But Barbara's voice from the stage dragged me away for just an instant, and what Mark said eluded me once more.

Well, whatever he had said was meant to put me at ease, that was clear enough. "Thanks," I whispered, and somehow I managed to smile at him. "I guess I'm next."

But a wave of hopelessness swept over me.

How could I try out for the part of Nora Helmer, for the lead role? I couldn't trust myself enough anymore. If I couldn't even hear Mark, how could I ever hope to follow all the action on the stage? In some of the scenes several people would be on stage all at once, talking and tossing out cues I would have to snatch without an instant of hesitation. The slightest mistake I made would throw everyone else off balance.

"All right, Barbara, that'll be enough," Mrs. Ikeda called. "Jody, I guess you're the last one to read for Nora. Then I'll cast the minor parts."

My knees shook as I got to my feet. "Mrs. Ikeda, I — I think I better not. I . . ."

But then I saw the look on Mark's face, a blend of dismay, bewilderment, and was it irritation? I was trapped. If I backed down now he would know for certain that something was wrong. "I think I'd rather try out for one of the smaller parts," I pleaded. "I'm kind of busy and — I just think it'd be better."

Mrs. Ikeda nodded. "Sure, you can read for the part of Nora's friend, Christine Linde. Start over on page fourteen with her entrance."

I felt light-headed as I walked to the front of the auditorium and mounted the three steps to the stage. Mrs. Ikeda had a deep, clear voice that carried well. I had no trouble hearing her as she read my cue lines, and I answered her, my own voice sounding strangely small as it floated out over the enormous room. Mrs. Linde was supposed to appear dejected and tired according to the stage directions. I let my shoulders slump, let my words fall slowly and heavily. I felt weary and discouraged enough myself to step right into the character.

"Fine," Mrs. Ikeda said when I had reached the bottom of the page. "Skip over to Act Three. I'll read Krogstad's lines."

Was it only my imagination, or had I detected a note of approval in her brisk "Fine"? I found the spot at the beginning of Act Three and began to read again. Christine Linde was more animated by now. Her words were earnest and intense. I was feeling better by now myself as I caught each cue Mrs. Ikeda threw to me. My shoulders lifted and new energy found its way into my voice.

I read a page and a half before Mrs. Ikeda held up her hand to stop me. "Okay, that's enough. Who else would like to read for this part, for Christine Linde?"

I was heading back to my place next to Mark as Mary Jo climbed onto the stage. I hadn't even realized that she had come this afternoon.

"Why didn't you go for the lead?" Mark demanded even before I sat down. "I thought —"

"Oh, I just changed my mind, that's all." It was a pretty lame excuse and I knew it.

"I just don't get it," Mark persisted. "I thought you really wanted it. You kept studying those scenes and everything."

"Yeah, but then I heard Barbara read," I told him. "I couldn't do any better than her. I figured I'd have a better chance if I —"

"Shsh!" hissed Barbara from her seat at the far end of the row. Mark and I fell silent as Mary Jo began to read. She read with exaggerated emotion, hamming it up.

I'd probably hit upon the only explanation Mark might accept. After all, he knew how impressed I'd been by Barbara's performance as Elizabeth. It was only natural that I'd feel I couldn't compete with her.

I'd escaped awkward questions once more. But a doubt nagged in the back of my mind. Would I really be able to protect my secret forever? Or, like Nora Helmer, would I be forced to reveal the truth in the end?

I got up early the next morning, gulped a glass of orange juice and dashed off to school. Somehow I needed to walk there alone, without Mark or Nancy or someone else. When I read the cast list on the bulletin board outside the main office, I didn't want anyone to be watching me.

I still wasn't quite sure what I wanted to find. I longed for a part in the play, but at the same time I almost hoped that my name wouldn't appear on the list. Then I could slip into the background again, where I could be safe and anonymous, where I wouldn't have to take any chances.

I arrived at school so early that the list wasn't even posted yet — my anxiety again. For a few moments I just gazed at the bulletin board, covered with outdated announcements. Then I turned away and began to pace. I wandered up to my locker, back down past the library, strolled by the boys' locker room, and finally doubled back to the main office and the bulletin board again.

And as if by magic the list had appeared. It was tacked in the upper lefthand corner, the words A DOLL'S HOUSE marching boldly across the top. I stepped closer and scanned the column of names: "Torvald Helmer, Fred Margolis . . . Nora Helmer, Barbara Kalajian . . . Christine Linde, Jody Chase . . ."

I stood there in a trance, reading my name over and over. It was settled now. Whether I wanted it or not, the role of Christine Linde was mine.

Suddenly I was aware that someone had come up beside me. I turned and saw Barbara, her face glowing with excitement. Right behind her stood Mary Jo.

"Congratulations!" I cried. "You're Nora! That's fantastic!"

"Congratulations to you, too," Barbara exclaimed. Impulsively she flung her arms around me, and we were both talking at once. The doubts that had pursued me as I paced the halls were all gone now. I had a part! I was Christine Linde!

"I'll have to start thinking of you as Christine," she giggled. "My old buddy from school."

"Nora, old friend!" I exclaimed, and returned her hug.

By now other people were crowding around, edging in to get a look at the list. I saw Kathy Ferone turn away, biting her lip with disappointment. Mary Jo was saying, "Well, looks like I'm the maid again. My usual part."

"Oh, it's not such a bad part," I told her. "The maid comes into practically every scene."

"Sure, I guess so." But she didn't look convinced. She added grudgingly, "Well, congratulations, Jody. Hey, maybe I can be your understudy, in case you get too busy or get sick or something."

What did she mean by that, anyway? Did she think I might drop out of school next week to go into a home for unwed mothers?

Well, she'd see that there was nothing the matter with me. I had a part in *A Doll's House* — not the lead, but a good solid part I could work with — and nothing was going to stop me now.

Then one thought drove all the others out of my head. I glanced at my watch. There were still ten minutes before the first bell would ring. If I ran I'd have plenty of time.

I said good-bye to Barbara and Mary Jo and raced up Stairway D to the Chemistry lab. Mark and Mr. Lopez bent over a rack of glass beakers. But Mark spotted me the moment I stepped through the doorway.

"You made it!" he cried. "I can tell just by looking at you."

"I can still hardly believe it," I exclaimed. "You were right — I did it. I'm Christine Linde, and we start rehearsing tomorrow night."

THIRTEEN

Mr. Prendergast had the habit of pacing back and forth in front of the classroom, from the door to the windows, from the windows to the door. But I couldn't afford to be lulled by his slow, measured steps. We were ten minutes into the period and I still hadn't answered a question.

By the desk Mr. Prendergast paused to polish his glasses. Then he paced on to the door and turned back. ". . . has been said there are parallels . . . Andrew Johnson's administration and our own recent times," he said. He tended to mutter, looking down at the floor, and I really had to strain to understand him. ". . . and a lot of differences, too. Who can tell me, what era am I thinking of?"

This was my chance. My hand shot up and I gazed at him imploringly, willing him to call on me.

"Jody?" he asked.

"Watergate," I said. "The Watergate Era. The way Nixon had to resign, it's kind of like how they tried to impeach Andrew Johnson."

Mr. Prendergast nodded. He resumed his pacing and his lecture. I settled back in my seat. Now that I had volunteered an answer I was relatively safe. Mr. Prendergast wasn't likely to call on me unexpectedly this afternoon. With the way he mumbled, sometimes even half turned away from the class, I was always afraid he would call on me when I had missed the question or hadn't quite heard some key phrase that led up to it.

That was one of the little tricks I'd learned over the past few weeks. It worked in most of my classes, except in English, where Miss Laurier liked to lead "stimulating discussions." There were times I'd lose track of what was going on, when everyone got talking at once. But I could usually throw in a comment after some deep-voiced boy who was easy to understand, just to be on the safe side.

I was doing better in the cafeteria lately, too. I just didn't talk as much as I used to. By now it seemed natural to sit quietly over my lunch, nodding when I didn't quite know what the others were talking about.

There were still snags once in a while, though, like today when Nancy asked if anyone had seen Connie's dumb get-up. All I caught were a few fragments of the question, just enough to make me think she had asked, "Can I have some catsup?" There was some on my tray, one of those little plastic envelopes that came with my hamburger, so I handed it to her across the table.

Nancy just looked blank and asked, "What's this for?" And I got a cold, sinking sensation in my stomach, the horrible feeling that I had made a big mistake.

It was time to act, I told myself, and plunged in with a light little giggle. "Oh, isn't that what you wanted?" I asked.

"I said, had anyone seen Connie's dumb get-up," Nancy repeated loud enough for her voice to pierce through the noise in the background. "This weird long green dress — didn't you hear me?"

"Oh, you know me," I said. "My mind is always drifting off."

"You're going to be America's first woman in space," Barbara said. We all laughed, and the talk moved on to something else.

Maybe I was acquiring a new image. But I didn't mind much if people decided I was spacey. It was a lot better than having them know that I was handicapped, wasn't it?

But when I was rehearsing for *A Doll's House* I knew I was in control. I might lag behind in the repartee backstage, but when I stepped into my role as Christine I felt a surge of confidence. I had been the first to know all my lines, studying them in every spare moment until they flowed without effort. I tried to put all of Mrs. Ikeda's directions to use, and in front of my mirror at night I practiced being Christine — Christine feeling dejected and weary, Christine conspiring to help Nora keep her secret, Christine revealing her love for Krogstad at last. At first I didn't feel the bond of sympathy with Christine that I had discovered with Nora. But as the days passed I was coming to know her better and better.

Just as I had suspected, conversing in the play was in some ways easier than talking to people in real life. I knew in advance precisely what everyone around me was going to say. From the beginning I had little trouble hearing my cues. Fortunately Mrs. Ikeda insisted that everyone on stage had to project. "I'm the deaf lady with the hearing aid sitting in the back row," she would say. "If I can hear you, then you know you're doing all right." So everyone in the cast spoke out loud and clear, even Barbara, whose light, high-pitched voice otherwise faded in and out of my range.

Sometimes I could almost laugh aloud. It seemed so ironic that Mrs. Ikeda was pretending to be a deaf lady in the back row, while the real deaf person was right on stage. Probably she wouldn't have ever given me a part in the play if she had known I had a hearing problem. But I was doing fine, and she would never even guess.

". . . many enemies in the Congress," Mr. Prendergast droned. ". . . an attempt to undermine . . ."

I dragged my thoughts back to History. Once I had been able to daydream through my classes, listening with half an ear just in case a random question came at me by surprise. But now I didn't let my attention waver. I'd answered one question and I was pretty safe. But I couldn't afford to take chances.

The bell rang at last and another school day

was over. I gathered up my books and joined the scramble for the door. Finally, I could relax. Walking home alone I could let my mind wander as much as I wanted.

But Mark was waiting for me by my locker. "Hey," he said, "practice was called off this afternoon. I'll walk you home, okay?"

"Great," I exclaimed. I wouldn't be able to relax completely on the walk home after all, I thought as I twirled the combination and pulled open my locker door. But that didn't matter. Being with Mark was worth the sacrifice.

The days were starting to grow longer, and we stepped out into a clear, sunny afternoon. We took the long way home, walking slowly down quiet side streets, and Mark told me about his science project and the basketball team and what a pest his little sister Lisa was becoming. There wasn't much traffic once we got off Wilmer Avenue. It was easy to hear everything he said, and to respond without falling back on silly giggles for support.

Mom was out when we got to my house. She had left a note on the dining room table, explaining that she was at a meeting of the AAUW Scholarship Committee. But there was a letter for me in the rack in the front hall, and the thin airmail envelope told me at once that it was from Mavis in England.

I took it from the rack and automatically began tearing it open. Then I remembered. Mavis knew.

"Is that from your pen pal?" Mark wanted to

know. "You really write a lot, don't you? What do you ever find to say to each other?"

"Oh, nothing much." I led him into the kitchen and got out a couple of Cokes and a bag of pretzels.

"Oh, you must write about something," Mark persisted. "It must be kind of interesting or else you wouldn't keep it up. Like what does she say in this letter?"

"I don't know. I'll read it later." It was definitely time to change the subject. "Are you going to have time to help out backstage with the play again? You know, on the sets and everything?"

Mark shrugged. "I figure I'll come help out during the last week. That's when things are always the most hectic. They'll be able to use some extra hands then, I guess."

The letter lay face down on the table in front of me. My eyes kept straying back to it as we sat and talked. Would Mavis feel differently about writing to me now that she knew I had a hearing problem? I'd felt a burning need to tell someone when I wrote to her, but I wasn't sure I wanted to read her answer now. Yet at the same time I had to know what she would say.

After a while Mark said he wanted to use the phone. He had to make some arrangements with Ted Davidson from the basketball team. I snatched up the letter the moment he stepped out into the hall.

"*Dear Jody,*" Mavis began. "*Thanks so much for your last letter. We've had terrible rains here and spring can't come soon enough to suit me.*

I've been thinking a lot about the trouble you're having with your hearing . . ."

Mark's shadow fell across the doorway and I thrust the letter hastily aside. "That was quick," I said brightly. "Wasn't he home?"

"I left him a message." Mark took his seat again and reached for a handful of pretzels. His glance flickered toward the letter and he couldn't have helped noticing that the envelope was torn completely open now. But to my relief he didn't ask any more awkward questions.

I thought of Nora Helmer. Once she had gotten some work doing copying to help pay off her debt, and her husband never found out. She'd shut herself up in her room to work and pretended she was busy making Christmas ornaments to surprise him. I knew how Nora must have felt. Like her I was constantly weaving tales that would conceal the truth. And I was growing better and better at it every day.

At last Mark said he had to get home or he'd be late for dinner. I walked with him to the front door. "You want to go to a movie Saturday night?" he asked me as he collected his books.

"Sure. What's playing?"

"There's one of those horror pictures out at the mall. But there's another one there, too, something with Burt Reynolds, I think."

"It's a waste taking me to those horror shows," I said. "I spend half the time hiding my face."

"Well, we'll go to something," Mark promised. "Consider yourself booked up for Saturday night."

He opened the door. Then he turned back, put his hand on my shoulder, and kissed me good-bye. "Parting is such sweet sorrow," he said, grinning.

"That I could say good night till it be morrow," I finished.

Things between us were still as good as they had ever been. The future stretched before us, an unbroken chain of times we would share, warm and shining. I would never have to feel Mark's pity. I would never have to sense that I had become an embarrassment to him.

I went back to the kitchen and unfolded Mavis's letter again.

". . . I've been thinking a lot about the trouble you've been having with your hearing. It must be awfully hard, and maybe you really ought to see a doctor straight away. You know, they might be able to do something. Anyway, it would be worthwhile to go and find out, don't you think?"

Minnie sprang onto my lap. She reached up to bat at the page with a dainty paw. I set the letter down and stroked her soft, sleek fur. Minnie's purr tingled through my fingertips in rumbling waves. Why did people talk about the sound of a cat's purr? A purr was a vibration to be felt rather than heard.

Of course what Mavis said made sense. Maybe I really ought to see a doctor. Maybe I would find out that my hearing could improve again.

But whenever I thought of going to a doctor I came to the same dead end. Suppose the doctor told me I had waited too long? Besides, I wasn't really worried about my hearing anymore. I was getting along fine now.

Minnie jumped to the floor and I picked up the letter again.

"There's a girl named Jane Hargrove in my form who is hard of hearing, but when you're with her you forget all about it. She's very good in her studies and she plays excellent tennis. You don't even have to speak up for her because she wears a hearing aid and she can understand everything almost perfectly. So really you shouldn't be afraid to tell anyone. I think if it were me I would feel just as you do at first. But I couldn't keep it all inside me for very long; that would drive me mad.

"I'm studying very hard now for my A-Levels. The examinations aren't till June but it's all terribly important . . ."

I read to the end of the letter, but I could hardly keep my mind on Mavis's exams and Nigel, the new boy she liked. I kept thinking of poor Jane Hargrove, destined to struggle through life with a hearing aid. It must be awful to walk around hooked up to a weird-looking gadget like that. Sure, Mavis claimed that Jane was just like everybody else. But how could she be when she was so obviously different? Did the other kids at school like her, or were they only trying to be nice?

Mavis thought she would go mad trying to keep a secret like mine. But she couldn't really understand what was at stake. I had friends, I acted in plays, and Mark van Huysen was my steady boyfriend. I had so much, and I couldn't risk losing it all.

Usually I saved Mavis's letters. But I didn't want to leave this one lying around. Not that Mom or Dad ever read my mail — but still, I couldn't take any chances.

Slowly I tore the crisp airmail sheets into tiny bits. I opened my hands over the wastebasket and they drifted down like snowflakes. "So much for doctors and hearing aids," I told Minnie.

But Minnie only stretched and blinked and went back to washing her paws.

FOURTEEN

"Your hands are freezing," Mark said softly. He tried to rub some life into them, but it was no use. All around us people hurried and whispered, and out on the stage Barbara and Fred, as Nora and her husband, were already deep into the opening scene of the play. Out there the rows of seats would be crowded with spectators. The audience watched and listened and judged.

I knew that everyone was there tonight. Dad had gotten back from a trip to Chicago this morning and Kim was home on spring break from college. So the whole family had bought tickets. And Nancy had promised to come with Connie and Sylvia and as much of the Secret Society as she could muster. And of course Mrs. Ikeda was out there somewhere. Had I really learned everything she'd tried to teach me? Or would I disappoint her in the end?

Through the weeks of rehearsal my confidence had soared. But now, as I stood backstage with Mark on opening night, my hands had turned to ice, and I was getting a classic attack of butter-flies in the stomach.

"Stage fright?" Mary Jo paused beside us in the black dress that served as her maid's costume.

"I'll get over it," I said, straightening my shoulders. "I'll just make believe it's another rehearsal."

"I'm not scared at all, but I've had more experience," Mary Jo said, but she toyed nervously with the white lace at her wrist. "This'll be a piece of cake."

"We better get set," I told her. "We go on in a minute."

Mark gave my hand a parting squeeze and Mary Jo and I went to stand by the door stage left. On the stage Nora and her husband talked about Christmas presents and a tree, and how much easier their life would be now that he had a better job at the bank.

And then it was time. Mark, who was in charge of sound effects, rang the bell, and Mary Jo stepped onto the stage to announce my arrival.

"Ask her to come in," Nora said, and Mary Jo turned back and ushered me out onto the stage.

Mrs. Ikeda had warned us not to be intimidated by the audience. But in that first moment, when I looked out over the sea of faces, something tightened in my chest and I could hardly breathe. Mom and Dad and Kim smiled proudly at me, and farther back I glimpsed Nancy's hand lifted in salute. And Mrs. Ikeda and her husband must be sitting out there somewhere, though I couldn't spot them. Everyone waited for me to speak.

I opened my mouth but no words would come out. My mind was a blank. What was I doing out here, anyway? This was all an awful mistake.

Then somehow I brought Nora into focus. I heard myself say, "How do you do?" in a strange, wooden voice that wasn't quite my own.

We were alone in this scene. I stood in front of Nora, dressed in a dark woolen skirt, a coat draped over my arm. It was winter, it was almost Christmas, and I had come a long way today, all the way from my little hometown, though I had no idea what I would find in the city. I was dejected and tired after my long journey, and I desperately needed a friend. I was Christine Linde.

"How do you do?" Nora asked doubtfully. And I answered, "You don't recognize me, I suppose."

"No, I don't know — yes! Christine, is it really you?"

Someone in the audience coughed, but Barbara was projecting beautifully. I could hear every word. My own lines leaped into my mind exactly when I needed them.

Nora asked me to sit down and I hung my coat on the back of a chair. I listened to her account of the past ten years, asking her questions to draw her out. Then I began to tell her the sad tale of my own life.

After all the studying and rehearsals this was the real performance at last. Here I stood on the stage, bringing my lines to life. Now I had to give it everything I had.

The scene unwound swiftly. Soon I had said all I was meant to say. It was time for me to make my exit, to rush backstage and change my clothes, to peer into the mirror and make certain that my make-up was still all right.

Mark was waiting to greet me. "Great," he whispered close to my ear. "Beautiful."

"Thanks," I said. I was still caught up in the play, and I felt as though this bit of time backstage was just a short interval before I would spring to life again. And I knew deep within myself that I was doing well.

At the end of *The Barretts of Wimpole Street* I had sat alone backstage, wistfully picturing how it would be to go out for the curtain call. Well, after the curtain fell on *A Doll's House* I found out that it was just as triumphal as I had imagined. There we stood, every one of us, bowing and smiling. And I certainly had no trouble hearing the applause.

Through the performance we had all worked together with discipline and determination. But the moment our curtain call was over all order disintegrated. Fred Margolis let out a wild whoop, and then we were all laughing and talking at once. Even Mary Jo threw her arms around me and cried, "We did it, Jody! We really did it!"

"There's still another show tomorrow night," Barbara pointed out as we swarmed backstage. "This was just kind of a second dress rehearsal."

Mark rushed forward and swept me into a joyful hug. "Jody, you were fantastic! In that scene at the end, your love scene, you were practically heart-rending."

"It really got to me somehow this time," I said excitedly. "All of a sudden it really hit me how she'd loved him years ago, and all those years she'd been miserable because she'd made a terrible mistake . . ."

". . . hot out there!" Fred exclaimed. "All those sweating bodies in the audience . . ."

". . . pictures during Act Two?" someone demanded. "I thought Mrs. Ikeda said absolutely no . . ."

". . . better look at that door on the left . . . Loose enough to fall off the set . . ."

". . . tomorrow'll be worse — they say the second show . . ."

"Yeah, break a leg, everybody!"

I couldn't understand everything everyone was saying, but in that confusion it didn't make any difference. Somehow I found my jacket and purse, and Mark and I edged our way outside. Mom, Dad, and Kim waited for us by the stage door, beaming and waving and calling their congratulations.

"I'm really impressed!" Kim exclaimed. "You were as good as some of the kids in the drama group at college."

I could hardly believe I had heard her right. Kim was the intellectual of the family, the perfectionist who set impossible standards for herself and everyone else around her. I waited for her to add some bit of "helpful criticism" which would show just how much she knew about the theater, and about Ibsen in particular. But none came. Maybe college was having a good influence on her.

"I baked a chocolate cake," Mom said when the flurry of congratulations was over. "You're coming back with us, aren't you, Mark?"

"Sure," Mark said. "I never turn down chocolate cake."

So we all clambered into the station wagon and Dad drove us home. He said he thought he was suffering from jet lag, and Kim complained that she couldn't find a thing since Mom had been rearranging her room. But they kept coming back to how much they had enjoyed the play, and how convincingly I had acted my part in it.

Mark and I trailed Mom into the kitchen and she unveiled the cake. I don't know where she'd found the time to bake it. She'd had a class all morning and had dashed off to some committee meeting right after lunch. But there it stood, covered with glorious swirls of chocolate icing, a monument to my success.

Kim was telling Dad some story about a problem with her car, but they broke off when we came in. "Oh, boy, that looks delicious!" Dad exclaimed. "For this special occasion — Jody's play and Kim's homecoming."

"Right," Kim said. "Better not leave me out. You don't want to stir up any sibling rivalry, do you?" Ever since she decided to major in psychology, Kim was always throwing around terms like that.

"Well, if you want to know the truth, it was really inspired by the Scholarship Committee," Mom said, laughing. "Our area chapters raised forty thousand dollars —"

"Forty thousand!" I cried. "That's tremendous. I mean, how could you?"

"Not *forty* thousand," Mom said, shaking her head. "Don't I wish! *Fourteen* thousand."

"Oh, well," I said, and managed to dismiss the subject with a giggle. "Fourteen thousand is still a lot."

"So how does it feel to be a star?" Dad asked. "Were you nervous up there?"

"Oh, just at first. Then it got going real smoothly. Except in Act Two, remember that part where I was helping Nora mend her party dress? I was sitting there sewing, and all of a sudden I realized I had stitched the dress right to my skirt! It was a good thing I noticed just in time. I worked like crazy and got the stitches all out . . ."

Everybody laughed, and Mom said, "You certainly didn't let on there was a crisis. You carried it off like a pro."

Mark sat down on the sofa beside me and handed me a slice of cake on a saucer. "You know, it was fun working the sound effects, but I hated missing your performance. You've got to be in something else so I can have the chance to watch you from the audience."

I was glowing with confidence. I knew that for me tonight was only a beginning. "I'll try," I assured him. "I wonder what they'll put on next fall."

Dad finished his cake and said something about putting on the news.

"Don't turn the TV up too loud," I said casually. "Just leave it kind of low so we can talk."

He glanced at me in surprise. "What's the matter? Usually you're the one who puts it up to two hundred decibels."

"Sure, but I don't want to listen to it now. I mean, I just want to talk to everybody." I said it so lightly and easily that no one in the room would guess how important it was.

Dad switched on the set. "That ought to be low enough for you," he said. The newscaster's voice was only a quiet murmur.

I nodded my thanks and Dad sat down again. Mark and I discussed plans for the cast party tomorrow night, and occasionally I caught snatches of the conversation between Mom and Kim.

I saw Dad first straighten up in his chair, then lean forward, becoming more and more absorbed in the news. He grimaced as though he had heard something thoroughly unpleasant, but I couldn't follow what the announcer was saying at all.

"Those rats!" Dad exclaimed, thumping his fist into his open palm. "They just raised taxes this year. Now they want a new sales tax!"

"I don't understand why you watch that," Mom remarked. "It just gets you upset every time."

"Indigestion," Dad muttered. "If they'd just put *me* in charge of the government for six months —"

"Indigestion?" I repeated. "Does it really give you indigestion, Dad, or are you just kidding?"

For an awful instant there was silence. I glanced from Dad to Mark, to Mom and Kim.

They were all looking at me oddly. I had said something wrong again.

"Who said anything about indigestion?" Dad said finally. "I said, 'That's a good question.'"

"Oh, well, you know me," I said brightly. "My mind's always wandering off some place."

"Are you sure your hearing is okay?" Mark asked. "Maybe —"

His words stung, but there wasn't time to let myself feel anything. "Well, watching the news could give you indigestion," I exclaimed. "All that blood and gore. Anyhow, Dad, what would you do if you ran the government for six months?"

"Well," Dad said, "first of all I'd replace all the top officials with . . ."

I glanced furtively at Mark while Dad talked. Had I managed to distract him, or was he still pondering my hearing? "Then what?" I asked. "What else?"

Dad leaned back and propped his feet on the hassock. He was beginning to get into the spirit. "I think I'd really put free enterprise into practice," he said. "No more bailing out these companies all the time."

"Wait, wait!" Mark held up his hand. For one terrifying moment I was certain what was going to come next. I tried to brace myself for Mark's words that would resound through the living room like a judge's gavel.

But Mark wasn't looking at me now. He faced Dad, his eyes lit with a mischievous sparkle. "Wait, are you in charge of the state or the federal government?"

"Oh, I may as well take over the federal government while I've got the chance," Dad said expansively. "So if these companies go under, they go under. And by the same token, if you want to set up a hot dog stand on Main Street you don't have to apply for a license or anything like that. You just get yourself some hot dogs and set up shop."

I was safe. Everything was going to be all right. I tried to breathe easily and normally again, tried to quiet the thudding of my heart. Mark hadn't meant anything by that question about my hearing. By now he'd forgotten all about it. I had managed to distract him, and now he was swept up in Dad's fantasy. He was saying something about putting bicycle paths along all the highways, and Mom was demanding free national health insurance. It was the sort of game Dad delighted in inventing. In another few minutes we'd all be shouting at one another as though we could really persuade him to put our ideas into practice.

Only Kim was quiet. She sat in the armchair by the fireplace, her hands folded on her lap, and the way she looked at me made me feel tense all over again.

"And disarmament," I threw in. "We could quit selling weapons to all those other countries, and dismantle all the bombs."

"We'll get the other countries to dismantle theirs first," Dad said. "Once they do it, then we'll do it, too."

Still Kim didn't join in. She sat very still, as though she were lost in thought.

Maybe she was just tired after her long trip. Or maybe she was observing us all and trying to apply the things she'd learned in her psychology classes. Probably from now on she'd be using us all as guinea pigs every time she came home.

But there wasn't time to sit and wonder what was going on in Kim's mind. I had to concentrate on what everyone was saying, and hurl myself into the debate. I had to keep up the act that I was perfectly normal.

"That's what they always say," I told Dad. "That's why we're in this whole mess. You're in charge, you've got the chance to do something,"

When I glanced back at Kim she was studying her nails as though there wasn't another thing on her mind.

FIFTEEN

It would be sensible to get my homework done this morning. With the second performance of the play tonight and the cast party afterward, it would be nice to have my assignments over with so I could sleep late tomorrow morning.

But when I opened my History book to Chapter Twenty-three I couldn't keep my mind on the assassination of President Garfield. I hadn't been to a party in almost three months, not since the cast party after *The Barretts of Wimpole Street*. I hadn't even gone to a meeting of the Secret Society for a while. I should plot out my strategy for survival before I got to the party tonight. Probably I'd be wise to mix a lot in the beginning, just giggling and acting scatterbrained if I didn't know quite what people were talking about. Then, after a decent interval, I could escape to the kitchen and make myself useful serving food or washing dishes. It would be quieter out there, and if I kept busy I'd hardly have to speak to anyone. I'd get through it somehow. I might even have a good time.

The doorbell rang just as I finally settled down to work. Probably it would be someone here to see Kim, I thought. Still I struggled to sift out the jumble of voices that floated up from the front hall — a woman, and the thin piping voices of children.

"Jody!" Mom called from the foot of the stairs. "Aunt Eva's here, with the kids.".

So much for history homework, I thought, snapping my book shut. Aunt Eva was Mom's younger sister, and whenever she dropped by with her two children they wound up staying for hours. Penny and Todd were cute and fun to be with, but as Mom always said, Eva had her hands full.

"Coming," I shouted, and started down the stairs.

Todd bounded halfway up the stairs to greet me, flinging his arms around my ankles and nearly tripping me up. He grinned to display the gap where his two front teeth used to be. "Jody," he cried. "I'm six now. Want to see my bubble pipe?"

"Not in the house," Aunt Eva warned. She turned to Mom and said something about how she hoped this was no inconvenience, just stopped in to say hello, coming from Penny's appointment with the speech therapist . . .

I caught sight of nine-year-old Penny, half-hidden behind her mother. She peered around the living room with big dark eyes. Kim came in from the den and her greetings added to the general confusion.

"We really can't stay long," Aunt Eva said. But she settled herself into the armchair and propped her feet up on the hassock. She looked as though she didn't intend to budge for a good long while.

"We were just about to have lunch," Mom said. "I'll just make some more sandwiches. We can eat buffet style, nothing formal."

". . . can I?" Todd was imploring me, tugging at my hand. "Please?"

"What?"

"Oh, we didn't expect you to feed us," Aunt Eva protested weakly. "Don't go to any trouble."

". . . upstairs!" Todd was saying. "Can't I? Like last time?"

"Can't you what?" I repeated. I bent closer and tried to catch his words.

By now he was growing impatient. "Your puppets!" he almost shouted. "Can't I play with them?"

"Oh, sure, if there's time after we have lunch." Todd had had a wonderful time playing with my puppets the last time they came to visit us. They were in a cardboard box at the bottom of my closet, leftovers from childhood that I couldn't quite bring myself to store in the attic. There was a rabbit and a bear, a lion, an owl, and a dragon whose jaws could open and shut.

Kim was trying to say hello to Penny, but Penny only smiled shyly and whispered something I couldn't hear at all.

"Don't be so shy," Aunt Eva told her sternly. "You know what Miss Rutherford told you this morning. You have to get over this." She turned to Mom and added, "Some of the other kids have been teasing her, and she's developed this fear of talking to people. She never used to be self-conscious about her stutter."

"Before lunch!" Todd was insisting. "There's plenty of time —"

But Aunt Eva was asking me something. I turned away from Todd and watched her, concentrating on her words. ". . . hear you're doing a play," she said, and waited for an answer.

"How did you hear that?" I asked. "Did Mom tell you already?"

Aunt Eva looked blank. "Tell me what?"

"Oh, you know, about the play. I thought you said . . ." That awful feeling seized me again. I had done something wrong. I was dropping through a bottomless hole . . .

"All I said was, 'How are you doing today?'" Aunt Eva said. "I guess it's hard to hear yourself think when we come over."

"Well, it is a little noisy," I said, relieved. How could anyone question that excuse? "I'm doing okay. I'm in a play at school, so I guess that's why it was on my mind."

"Where's your father?" Mom asked me. "Maybe you can track him down."

"I bet he's down in the basement," I told her. "I'll go see."

". . . the puppets," Todd wailed.

"Later," I told him. I hurried into the kitchen and fled down the basement stairs.

But it was only a temporary reprieve. Dad was puttering at his workbench, but he was all too willing to come upstairs for lunch. Reluctantly I trailed after him, wishing more than anything that I could run back up to my room and hide from the noise behind my History book.

Instead I tried out my party strategy. I retreated into the kitchen and helped Mom slap together a stack of sandwiches. From the living room Dad's voice rose and fell as he asked Aunt Eva polite questions. Aunt Eva giggled, and Todd's voice lifted in a wail of protest against some indignity.

Finally Mom surveyed the platter of sandwiches and said, "I guess we better summon the mob. They can use paper plates and take them out to the living room." She went to the doorway and hollered, "Come and get it!"

Lunch was even more chaotic than I had feared it would be. Everyone talked at once, and Dad switched on the television because there was a baseball game he wanted to watch. It was almost a relief when Todd spilled his glass of 7-Up on the carpet. I fled to the kitchen for a roll of paper towels and a few moments of peace and quiet.

As I wiped up the mess I noticed Penny. She had chosen a straight-backed wooden chair, the most uncomfortable seat in the room, and had dragged it to the far wall by the windows. There she sat, nibbling at her sandwich, silent and remote.

Well, why should she want to talk to anyone, I thought. Whenever she tried to speak her words came out fighting. I was so used to Penny's stuttering that I never thought about it much. But the kids at school probably teased her mercilessly.

Todd was boisterous and cheerful, but I'd always been fonder of quiet, sensitive Penny. Now I pulled the hassock over to her corner and sat down beside her. "Hey, Penny," I said. "After we clean up, Todd and I are going to play with my puppets. You want to play with us?"

Penny shook her head and looked away.

"Why not?" I persisted. But that was a dumb question. The only way you could hide a stutter would be to keep your mouth shut all the time.

Penny said something, but her words crept out in the barest whisper. They were lost beneath the voice of the baseball announcer and a peal of Aunt Eva's laughter.

"I didn't hear you," I told Penny. "Come on, you'd like to play with us, wouldn't you? I've got some other stuff up in my closet too — a bunch of books, stuffed animals."

Penny's face contorted with the effort of speaking. It strained forward, trying vainly to grasp her words.

"Penny, you've got to talk louder," I said. "I can't hear."

She looked at me warily. Maybe she thought I was trying to trick her into talking more.

"No, really, it's true," I told her. "My ears don't work too well — I really can't hear sometimes."

I hadn't planned to say it. Somehow the words just slipped out. I looked around quickly to be sure no one else had heard me. But Dad was engrossed in the game, Mom and Aunt Eva were laughing over something, and Todd was munching an apple and looking bored. Kim was nowhere in sight.

Penny was staring at me with something like awe. "You can't hear?" she repeated. This time her voice was loud enough, and she didn't even stutter.

Almost instinctively I put my finger to my lips. "Well, not perfectly," I said. "But it doesn't stop me from doing things. I mean, I still do whatever I want, you know?" Would Penny tell her mother? What had ever possessed me to tell her about my hearing? Well, even if she did say something, nobody would take her seriously. And maybe it would help her somehow, knowing that I had a problem, too.

"Jody!" Suddenly Kim was striding toward us. She stepped over Todd's outstretched feet and came to stand beside me. "Didn't you hear me? Mark's on the phone."

"Oh, yeah?" I got to my feet. "Guess I didn't hear you with all the noise in here." I turned back to Penny and added, "See you later."

I followed Kim out into the hallway. I thought I caught her giving me another of those funny searching looks as I lifted the receiver from the table and held it to my left ear.

"Hey, Jody," Mark's voice said. "You want me to pick you up tonight? Then after the show we can drive over to the party. Okay?"

"Sure. Good idea." The hallway was fairly quiet. And it was usually pretty easy to hear people over the telephone, just a single voice aimed directly at me without a lot of background noise.

"Okay," Mark said. "We're supposed to be over at school by seven. I'll come by around quarter of?"

"Sounds good," I said. "I made some dip to bring to the party."

"Oh, yeah? That good onion dip you make?"

"Yeah. I mean, I hope it's good."

When I went back into the living room Kim was settled on the couch with a magazine. She only glanced at me as I passed her. Probably that funny searching look had just been created by my own imagination.

SIXTEEN

It was nearly four o'clock by the time we waved good-bye to Aunt Eva and the kids. I went upstairs and put away the puppets Todd had left scattered on the floor. Then I sat down at my desk again. Mark was coming by at quarter to seven and I still hadn't even started my assignment.

But I was all too grateful for the interruption when there was a knock at my door. "Come in," I called, and Kim stepped into the room, pulling the door shut again behind her.

"Hi," I said, pushing my History book aside. "Boy, it's been hectic around here. I've hardly had a chance to talk to you since you got home." This would be a perfect opportunity to talk, too, up here in the quiet of my room.

"I know." Kim dropped onto the bed and crossed her legs. "I've been wanting to ask you something, but I haven't had the chance till now."

She wanted to borrow something, I thought —

my suede purse, or that yellow dress of mine she'd always liked so much, or maybe some money so she could go out tonight . . .

"Well," I asked, "what can I do for you?"

Kim hesitated. It had to be money, then. But it would have to be a pretty hefty loan to make her twist her hands together on her lap and stare down at the carpet that way.

"It's not exactly something you can do for me," Kim said slowly. "It's just — you know, I've been noticing — I got to wondering last night — Jody, can you hear all right?"

I jumped as though someone had come up behind me and put cold fingers on the back of my neck. "Sure," I exclaimed. "Why do you want to ask me that?"

"It's just — the way you've been acting." Now her eyes rose to study my face, to bore into my thoughts and drag out the truth. "Last night, and then today when Aunt Eva was here, it seemed like you couldn't follow what people said all that well."

I was on stage again. The curtain had risen and taken me totally by surprise. "Oh, you know me," I said, giggling. "Sometimes I'm just not too with it, I guess."

Kim frowned. "It seems like you keep misunderstanding people," she said. "Answering the wrong questions, that kind of thing."

Kim wasn't going to give up easily. This might have to be the performance of a lifetime.

"That happens to everybody once in a while," I said. "You know how it is when the whole crowd gets talking all at once."

"That's true, I guess." Kim was thoughtful for a moment and I almost dared to relax. I was doing all right even in this unrehearsed show. I had to distract her, get her to talk about her courses or the guys she was meeting at college.

"I guess that's true," Kim repeated. "Only, you couldn't even hear me before when I called to tell you that Mark was on the phone. I never knew you to miss a phone call from Mark. And besides, you're right-handed. So how come you hold the phone to your left ear?"

I was being buried under an onslaught of questions. I opened my mouth to toss back a good logical explanation, but suddenly I felt as though I'd forgotten my next lines. I was alone on the stage and the audience waited, but no more words would come to rescue me.

"It just struck me as kind of funny," Kim went on. "I wouldn't have thought much about it, but combined with everything else . . ."

"Look, I'm talking to you right now, aren't I? You can tell I hear you, right? So what if I don't always hear everything perfectly? What's the big deal? Maybe it's a little easier hearing the phone with my left ear sometimes, so what difference does that make?" Now my words just kept coming, but none of them were doing me any good. When I looked into Kim's face it was all too plain that she knew.

"Hey," she said when I trailed miserably to a stop. "I don't mean to be the Inquisition or anything. It just seems like maybe you're having a problem. Maybe, you know, maybe you could do something about it."

"Don't start all that big sister stuff with me!" I flared. "And you can cut out your psychology, too. You can just leave me alone!"

Tears stung my eyes. I jumped up and made a rush for the door.

"Jody, come on. Where are you going?" Kim cried. "Just cool it — sit down. I just thought we could talk, that's all."

I paused, my hand on the doorknob. I didn't have to sit and talk to Kim about all this. It was none of her business, anyway.

But if I walked away now, what would stop her from going straight to Mom and Dad? Nobody would take Penny seriously if she started saying that I couldn't hear — she was just a little kid. But they'd listen to Kim all right.

"All right. What do you want to talk about?" I asked grudgingly. I walked back and sat down on the foot of the bed.

"Well, for one thing, do Mom and Dad know about all this? Have they noticed anything?"

"I guess not," I said. "They never say anything, just tease me once in a while about daydreaming or something. That just shows you, it's no big deal. Most people don't even notice it."

"No, they wouldn't, I suppose," Kim said, half to herself. "They're around you every day, and it's probably been such a gradual change — but I hadn't seen you since Christmas. When did you start to think something was wrong?"

I didn't have to answer. Once I answered her I was admitting that I did have a problem, erasing all the work of the past months.

But Kim already knew that I didn't hear well. I couldn't pretend with her anymore. And maybe it would be a relief to tell someone the whole story.

I drew a deep quavering breath and began, "The first time I noticed it was at rehearsal for the play we put on back in February . . ." My voice sounded dead. But slowly, painfully, I told her about the flu and the night I woke up with the earache. I told her how the realization had grown little by little until that terrible night when I sat alone in my room and confronted the truth. I told her now I'd kept it a secret from Mom and Dad and everyone else, even from Mark.

"And everything was going fine till now," I said. Suddenly I couldn't hold back the tears. Sobbing I clutched at her hand and begged, "You won't tell anybody, will you? I couldn't stand it! It'd be awful! Please!"

Kim's arms folded around my shaking shoulders. She hugged me hard.

"Hey, don't get upset. It's okay. Everything's going to be all right."

"You know what'd happen if the kids at school ever found out," I babbled. "They'd think I was weird or something. I know the way they are. And if Mark ever found out, he probably wouldn't even want to be seen with me anymore."

"Listen," Kim pleaded. "I never said I'd tell anyone. I don't have the right to do that."

I drew away from her a little to get a better

look at her face. She looked calm and serious, like she meant what she was saying. My heart gave a little leap of joy.

But she hadn't finished yet. "I won't say anything. But maybe you better start telling people yourself."

"No!" I cried. "How could I? I'd die! There's nothing really wrong with me, but people would treat me as if I were really deaf or something. Maybe they'd make me go to some special school even."

"Why should they do that? You're doing all right where you are," Kim said. "But you're wearing yourself out. You've got to work so hard all the time pretending you can hear. You must never be able to relax and be yourself."

She was right. It was exhausting. Sometimes by the end of the day I didn't want to have to speak to another soul. Once I had loved to spend hours with my friends, talking and giggling over nothing. Once I'd always been the first one to suggest a party. But all that seemed so long ago. I was a different person now.

Still, my friends had accepted the new me. I was quieter, I got confused sometimes, but I was still one of the gang.

Only how long would it be before Mary Jo dreamed up some fresh rumor? Next time she'd probably say I was taking drugs or something. Or when would Mom come home from one of her nursing classes, look at me, and suddenly snap all the facts into place? How long did I have before Mark would ask again, "Jody, can you hear all right?" and refuse to be distracted?

Kim leaned back against the wall, curling her legs beneath her. "It might not be as awful as you think," she went on, filling in the silence. "People just get used to things. They won't even think of it after a while. And anyway, Mark seems to me like the kind of guy who will just accept you the way you are. Don't underestimate him."

I studied Mark's picture taped above my mirror. He looked so relaxed, leaning against our back fence and grinning into the camera, as though nothing could ever bother him.

"Maybe he would," I said. "But you just can't tell about boys. Anyway, it'd be so awful if I saw a doctor and he said I waited too long after that earache."

"Maybe it doesn't have anything to do with your earache," Kim said. "I'm taking this course on exceptional children, and we had to read a lot about kids with hearing problems. Well, I got thinking last night how Mom always used to say you never heard her when she wanted you to do something around the house. And if I called to you from the next room, you'd always yell 'What?'"

"That's my motto these days," I said. "What? . . . Pardon? . . . Excuse me? . . ."

"In Cincinnati they say 'Please?'" Kim said. "That's where my roommate's from."

"Oh, good," I said. "I'll add that one to my repertoire for variety." I cupped my hand to my ear and said, "Please?"

"Come on, Jody, don't be facetious. I'm just saying maybe you had a hearing problem all your life but nobody ever realized it, and just lately it's gotten a little worse or something. But it's not your fault, for heaven's sake. And if you see an ear specialist, he can probably do something for you."

"Like give me a hearing aid," I said bitterly. "Some favor."

Kim straightened up and her feet hit the floor again. "Why should you care so much about what other people might possibly think? It's dumb to put yourself through all this, hiding from everybody. You've got to treat yourself better."

An image flickered across my mind — Penny hunched and silent on a chair by the far wall.

"Like you said, it's no big deal," Kim went on. "So why should people care one way or the other?"

I thought of Nora at the close of *A Doll's House.* When she faced her husband and told him the truth at last, she felt stronger, whole for the first time. "I can no longer content myself with what most people say," she told him. "I must think over things for myself and get to understand them."

"You think I should tell Mom and Dad," I said. They didn't sound like my own words, they came from so far away.

"They can call Dr. Ciccone," Kim said. "It'll be easy. He'll recommend a specialist and you'll go see him."

"It'll be so hard to tell them, though," I groaned. "They'll be mad because I didn't tell them a long time ago."

Kim didn't argue with that. She didn't offer any suggestions to make it easier, either. "It's just going to get harder the longer you put it off," she said.

"Just let me think," I said. "I've got to get ready for the play tonight. Mark's coming to pick me up. But maybe I'll talk to them tomorrow."

For a second or two Kim hesitated, and I still clung to the hope that I could get out from under all of this and go my own way again. Then she took command. "No," she said. "You better not put it off till tomorrow. If you're going to tell them, you better go downstairs and tell them right now."

I can't say that Kim forced me to go. She'd promised that she wouldn't tell anyone and I knew she'd keep her word. But I knew too that the time was up.

Slowly I stood up. "Okay," I said. "I don't know how I'm going to say it, exactly, but I guess I better go tell them now."

SEVENTEEN

"I still just don't understand it." Mom twisted around on the front seat to face me. "If you were worried about your hearing all that time, why didn't you tell us?"

I half turned away to look out at the gray factories that slid past us. "I don't know. I guess I can't explain it very well." I'd tried, but somehow I couldn't put it all into words for her. It was just one of those things parents can't seem to understand.

At first that Saturday afternoon it had been a relief to pour out the story to Mom and Dad. I wouldn't have to struggle and pretend anymore. At last with them I could really relax again and be myself.

But Mom's reproachful questions had pursued me for the past two weeks. Why hadn't I told them? What had I been afraid of? Hadn't I realized how important it was to take care of my hearing? I knew that behind it all lay the reproachful questions she kept asking herself. Why hadn't she noticed long ago that something was wrong with me? With her nursing background, why hadn't she recognized the signs?

Luckily, Dad kept trying to point out that feeling bad wouldn't get us anywhere. What we had to do, he said from the very beginning, was get me to a specialist and find out what the problem really was. If Dad hadn't been around I don't know what I would have done.

Now he said something to Mom about the traffic holding us up and she turned back to answer him. I sat and brooded alone in the back seat.

I hadn't mentioned my problem to Nancy yet, and I still hadn't told Mark, either. I told myself there was no point bringing it up until I knew what the specialist would say. As long as I hadn't heard the worst, there was still hope.

As soon as I told Mom and Dad, events seemed to spin out of control. Mom called Dr. Ciccone who managed to squeeze me in on Monday afternoon because someone had canceled an appointment. After he tested my ears and checked for wax he said that my hearing was "down a bit." He referred us to an otologist, Dr. Crowell, "for a complete workup."

By the time I went for my first appointment with Dr. Crowell, Kim had already gone back to college. It didn't seem quite fair somehow that she had triggered all of this and then left me to flounder through it on my own, without even her moral support.

The "workup" required two visits to the Hearing and Speech Center in the city. Through two long sessions I sat helplessly while Dr. Crowell and his assistant audiologist, Ms. Marasek, fastened strange instruments to my head to measure bone conduction and nerve responses and things they never bothered to explain to me at all. They scribbled notes. They spoke to one another in low, serious voices. But every time I asked what the tests showed Dr. Crowell would say, "Wait till our final conference, young lady. When all the results are in I'll answer your questions."

So today he would answer all my questions. This afternoon we were going in for the final conference.

It was all grimly familiar — the half-filled parking lot, the whoosh of the revolving door, the faintly antiseptic smell in the corridors. I trailed after Mom and Dad as they homed right in on Suite A-14. The receptionist looked up, smiled, checked her book and said, "Dr. Crowell will be with you in just a few minutes." She said it the same way each time we came.

This time the waiting room wasn't as crowded as usual. An elderly man with thick glasses dozed over a newspaper, and a harried-looking mother tried to keep a restless little boy from wriggling out of his chair. I picked up an old copy of *Seventeen* and leafed through it, glancing at the pictures.

"Smile," Dad told me. "You look like you're ready for the firing squad."

I tried to smile, but I could tell it came out pretty thin.

"Come on," Dad said. "All we're going to do is talk. Talk never hurt anybody, right?"

"Wrong," I said. I knew Dad was trying to make me feel better, but the only person who could make me feel better right now would be Dr. Crowell, by announcing that my hearing was just as good as everybody else's.

I wondered why doctors and dentists always played that drippy music in their waiting rooms. Maybe it helped some people relax, but to me the syrupy rendition of "I Could Have Danced All Night" sounded like a ballad of doom.

Dad glanced from me to Mom and back at me again, trying to think of something light and witty to say. But there was no more time. A door opened at the far end of the waiting room, and the receptionist pointed the way. "Jody Chase — and family? Through there, please."

Slowly I got to my feet. I smoothed my skirt and carefully returned *Seventeen* to the magazine rack. Desperately I tried to think of a way to delay going in for a few more seconds. But already Mom and Dad had started across the room. I could only follow them out through the door, down the narrow hallway, into Dr. Crowell's conference room.

This wasn't the examining room where I had been before. It was an office with ample leather chairs and a broad glass-topped desk. Behind the desk, in a swivel chair, sat Dr. Crowell. One glance at the plastic smile he had put on for the occasion told me all I needed to know. It was not the smile of a man who was about to deliver good news.

"Sit down, sit down," he said, pointing out the empty chairs with quick, nervous gestures. "We have all this young lady's records right here. I want to say a few words first, and then" — he beamed his smile at me — "you may ask all the questions you like."

Numbly I sat down. Dr. Crowell's smile dimmed as he rifled through the folder on his desk. I had nothing to ask him now. I dreaded the moment when he would begin to speak.

My icy hands lay folded upon my lap. My gaze wandered over the bookcases that lined the opposite wall, and I wondered if Dr. Crowell had a copy of *Hearing and Hearing Impairments*. I studied the framed diploma above his desk. So he had gone to the University of Rochester . . .

"Yes," he said at last. "I want you to listen very carefully. We've conducted a complete battery of tests and they show that this young lady" — he flicked on his smile for an instant and flashed it in my direction — "has a mild bilateral deficit. That is to say, to be more specific, a deficit of twenty decibels in the left ear and thirty-five in the right. Now these test have completely ruled out any middle ear involvement —"

His words rattled around me like hailstones. It was as though he had suddenly lapsed into a language as foreign as the Latin inscription on his diploma. *Bilateral deficit . . . bone conduction . . . audiogram. . . .*

But Mom and Dad nodded and murmured as though they understood him perfectly. "Yes," Mom said. "Yes, of course — if you've ruled out the middle ear it must be —"

"The inner ear," Dr. Crowell finished for her. "Yes, exactly. What we're dealing with here is a sensorineural impairment."

They were discussing me as though I weren't in the room at all. Well, maybe that's how they always treated people who had impairments. And part of me wanted to huddle in my chair, passive and uncomprehending.

Still, I might be impaired, but I had a right to understand my own fate. "What do you mean?" I burst out. "Explain all this to me. Am I going deaf or what?"

They all turned and stared at me.

"Jody, let the doctor finish," Mom began hastily.

But Dad broke in. "Yes, Doctor, maybe you could go over this again — in layman's terms, so we can all be more clear."

Dr. Crowell sighed like a teacher who has just been interrupted by a very silly question from the back row. He tried to put on a fresh smile but his mouth twitched with impatience. "All right, let me backtrack a little. Now, our tests have eliminated the possibility of a problem in the middle ear . . ."

"Please!" My voice rose almost out of control. "Can't you just tell me straight? Is there really something wrong with my hearing?"

Dr. Crowell looked at me for a long moment. He drew a deep breath. "Yes," he said. "Yes, I'm afraid there is."

The room swayed around me. I gripped the arms of my chair as Dr. Crowell's words came on, slow and steady and unrelenting.

"You have a hearing loss in both ears, but it's a bit worse in the right ear. In your type of loss there tends to be a certain amount of distortion of sound, so you might have difficulty understanding speech when there is a lot of background noise. Your greatest deficit — by that I mean a lack, a loss — is in the upper registers. That means it's harder for you to hear high notes, high-pitched voices, that sort of thing. Now, it's difficult to pinpoint the etiology . . ."

"Yes," I heard myself saying. "Girls' voices are harder to hear than boys'. And my right ear's always worse."

"But what could cause this?" Mom demanded, her face taut with anxiety. "If we had realized sooner . . ."

"I was just getting to that. The etiology, the cause." Dr. Crowell tapped a pen on the desk blotter. "It's almost impossible to pin down the cause in cases like this. A sensorineural loss is very often present from birth. Now, my suspicion is that your daughter has had a mild hearing loss all her life. It may have taken another dip recently, but I think we're dealing here with a congenital loss — a loss present at birth."

"No, that couldn't be," Mom protested. "We would have noticed, we would have . . ."

"She has always liked to turn the TV up louder than the rest of us wanted it," Dad said slowly. "And you know how we always kidded her about being a daydreamer. All those times we'd call her and she never seemed to be listening."

And I was only half listening now as they talked on about all the early signs of my hearing loss, signs they had misinterpreted and brushed aside. My mind was reeling. At last I broke in and asked, "You mean, all this isn't on account of that earache I had a couple months ago?"

Dr. Crowell tilted back in his chair. "Well, it's hard to say for sure. Sometimes people have a congenital loss and it will seem to get worse after some illness. But sometimes these losses just fall to a new plateau for no reason we can understand. It's just programmed to happen."

"Then if I'd come to see you right away after I had that earache, it wouldn't have made any difference?"

Dr. Crowell shook his head. "I'm afraid not. As I was saying, you have what we call a sensorineural loss, which means it's a problem in the inner ear. And medical science just hasn't advanced that far yet."

"Oh, thank goodness," I breathed. I guess that sounded pretty crazy. Dr. Crowell's eyebrows shot up and he gave me a very peculiar look. "I mean I was worried, because I didn't come right away," I stammered.

I don't think Dr. Crowell really understood what I was talking about. He glanced at his watch and went on where he had left off. "The point is," he said, "you've been compensating all your life. You never heard perfectly, so you never knew the difference. You just learned all sorts of ways to use your residual hearing — that's the hearing you do have."

"What's the prognosis?" Mom asked. She was trying to act calm but she kept fastening and unfastening the clasp of her purse.

"We'll have to check her hearing every few months for a while," Dr. Crowell said. "In a lot of cases the condition stabilizes at a plateau like this. In other words, her hearing may never get much worse than it is now. Or it may gradually get worse by the time she's middle-aged. But it's very unlikely that she'll ever be completely deaf."

"Well, that's a relief," Dad said. "Where do we go from here? What can be done?"

"I'm going to refer you back to Ms. Marasek. She's one of the best audiologist we have here at the Center. She'll try to fit this young lady with the best possible aid."

The room was quiet and I heard the words; Dr. Crowell projected beautifully. But somehow the meaning didn't reach me until Mom asked, "You mean a hearing aid?"

Dr. Crowell nodded. "She doesn't need a very strong one. Her loss is really within the mild range. But I think it would help, at school, for instance —"

"No!" I cried. "I don't need a hearing aid. Everybody could see it — what would people think? I won't use it."

"You know," Dr. Crowell said, "a lot more people wear hearing aids than you realize. They're made so compact nowadays they just tuck right behind your ear. The way you wear your hair, down like that, no one could even see it."

"But I don't need it," I repeated. "I'm doing okay in school. I can hear well enough."

Dr. Crowell turned to Mom and Dad. "We always see a bit of resistance in patients her age at first," he said. "But they get over it. Once she gets her aid she'll discover how much more she can hear with it. I think she'll be amazed at the improvement."

Oh, no, she won't, I wanted to scream at him. She gets along fine without any wires and contraptions and she isn't going to use any either so you can forget that idea . . .

Dad turned to me. He offered a brave smile. "You'll give it a try, won't you, Jody? To see if it helps you?"

"I won't have to wear one of those big ugly things like Aunt Dora's got?" I asked warily.

"No," Dad said firmly. "You heard what Dr. Crowell said. It'll be something very small and inconspicuous."

I didn't want to meet his eyes. They would demand a promise I wasn't ready to give. But he waited. No one spoke. And at last the long tingling silence compelled me to turn to Dad, to answer.

"All right," I said shakily. "If I really have to. I'll give it a try."

EIGHTEEN

"My, to what do I owe this honor?" Mom exclaimed when Dad suggested that he and I would do the dishes that night. It wasn't as if Dad never helped out in the kitchen at all, but he certainly didn't make a habit of it.

I had the uneasy feeling he had a reason for wanting me to help him. As we carried the dirty dishes out to the kitchen and tried to get things organized I braced myself for the lecture that was bound to come.

Dad held off until I'd started wrapping up the leftover chicken. "You know," he said, trying his best to sound offhand, "really I think finding out about your hearing problem is the best thing that could have happened."

"Sure. It's just terrific." I opened the refrigerator and busied myself shifting things around to make more room.

"No, I'm serious," Dad said. "Once you get used to the hearing aid I bet you'll be amazed at the change, just like Dr. Crowell said."

"Maybe." I scraped a couple of plates and switched on the dispose-all. For a few moments the grinding roar spared me from conversation. But as soon as I switched the machine off again, Dad made another try.

"All this time you've let people think you were — you know, kind of scatterbrained. Well, now they'll realize that you're not really like that at all. You can become your real self."

"I guess so," I said. "I just don't even know how I'm going to tell people — Nancy and Mark. But I'll have to let them know now. They'd figure it out soon enough anyway."

Dad leaned on the counter, his right hand hooked in his belt. "What you've got to do," he said, "is come across very matter-of-fact. Just act like it's no big deal. After all, lots of people wear glasses. A hearing aid is the same sort of thing."

I heard the phone ring out in the hall but I didn't move. "It's not the same," I said. "I know lots of people who wear glasses. I don't know one person who's got a hearing aid except Aunt Dora."

"But everybody's got some kind of a problem they have to overcome," Dad persisted. "Either they're too short or too tall, or their nose is too big, or they're not all that smart, or — well, everybody has something."

"Jody?" Mom had come to stand in the doorway. "Didn't you hear the phone? It's Mark."

"I heard it," I said. I wiped my hands on a towel and went out to the hall. For the rest of my life people would be asking me if I had heard things properly.

How was I going to speak to Mark? I longed to run up to my room, slam the door, and bury my head in my pillow. But my feet kept moving, my hand lifted the receiver from the table, and Mark's voice was clear and distinct in my left ear.

"Hi," he said. "How's everything? How come you had to leave school early this afternoon?"

"Oh, I had to — I had this —" I fumbled for words. "I had to go for a doctor's appointment."

"Oh, yeah?" Mark sounded concerned. "How was it? Are you healthy and all?"

"Sure," I said. "Sure, only . . ." Maybe I could still go on acting. It might take him weeks, even months to catch on.

"Only what?" Mark asked. "Is something the matter? You sound kind of weird."

"Do I?" I should have said it lightly, with the hint of a giggle to let him know it was nothing. But instead there was a catch in my throat. Then my words came out in a rush. "Mark, I've got to talk to you. Can you come over tonight?"

"Sure, I guess so. Can't you just tell me over the phone though? I've got all this Chemistry . . ."

"Please, it's really important. I need to see you."

"Okay," he said. "I'll be right over."

"It's not life and death or anything," I said hastily. "It's just that . . ."

"I'll drive. It's pouring out. I'll see you in about ten minutes."

"Thanks. See you."

Slowly I set down the receiver. I passed the

kitchen, where Dad was just starting the dish-washer. I avoided the living room where Mom had the television on as she read the evening paper. I went into the den and dropped onto the couch.

Waiting had never been an easy job for me. Generally I'd keep jumping up to look out a window or straighten a picture on the wall, or just to pace back and forth. But tonight I felt as if every drop of energy had been drained out of my body. I sat motionless, my hands locked together on my lap, and stared at the framed family photograph on the opposite wall. My time was up. I could never pretend to myself again that nothing was wrong. Dr. Crowell had set me straight on that. So if I didn't tell Mark now I would be living a lie.

But it wasn't fair! Nothing like this had ever happened to anybody I knew — not to Kim or Nancy or Mary Jo or anybody. Why was I the one to lose my hearing, to become handicapped? To be stuck wearing a hearing aid?

Minnie sprang up onto the couch beside me. She rubbed her head against my arm and stepped lightly onto my lap. As she settled down I stroked her gently and felt the vibration of her purr tingle through my fingertips.

Other people *heard* cats purr . . .

What else had I been missing? It was strange to realize that there were probably hundreds of tiny delicate sounds I had never heard all my life. When people talked about the rustle of branches overhead or the swish of grass as they walked through a field I'd always assumed they were just using figures of speech. But all those sounds must really exist, for other people.

Well, I'd lived sixteen years without rustling branches and swishing grass. Those things had never mattered before, so why should I care about them now? But they were part of the world. Now that I knew they existed, I knew I was being cheated.

Then my thoughts revolved back to Mark, out of my control. We had gone on our first date together June second of last year, doubling with Connie and a boy from out of town. Mark had encouraged me to try out for plays, and had made me beautiful things out of tiny bits of wood. We had played countless games of backgammon, and laughed at each other's jokes. In the summer we had gone for long bike rides. And in the winter we had driven up and down Wilmer Avenue searching for excitement, when all along the real excitement for us was just in being together.

Mark put up with my moods and shared my enthusiasms. Kim had said he seemed like the kind of guy who would accept me for myself, no matter what. But I didn't dare hope.

The doorbell rang. I set Minnie down on the floor and stood up slowly.

Mom was there ahead of me, greeting Mark with a broad smile, exclaiming over the rain outside and how he must be soaked through.

Mark smiled back and answered politely, but I thought he seemed a little worried. He watched me as I hung his dripping raincoat in the kitchen. At last Mom went back to the living room and we were alone.

"Well, what's going on?" Mark asked as soon as we were settled in the den. "You wanted to talk about something."

"Yes," I said. "It's about — this afternoon I went to — oh, it's so hard to explain!"

My mind leaped back to *A Doll's House*. I remembered how my throat had tightened when I stepped out onto the stage and saw the sea of expectant faces waiting to engulf me. But this was so much worse than stage fright!

"You had a doctor's appointment, right?" Mark said helpfully.

"Yeah. With Dr. Crowell. He's an ear doctor."

I waited for understanding to break like a storm across his face. But he only waited, his little half-smile inviting me to go on with the story.

"I already went two other times," I said. "They tested my hearing and all that stuff. And then today Mom and Dad went in with me for a conference with the doctor, you know. . . ."

I trailed off. Why couldn't Mark guess what I was going to say and spare me the agony of putting it into words for him? But he just sat quietly beside me on the couch and waited.

I took a deep breath and hurled the words into the space between us. "The doctor says I've got a hearing loss."

I don't know what I expected Mark to do — turn pale, maybe, and insist that it couldn't be true, there had to be some mistake, like someone on one of those TV doctor shows. But he didn't even wince. "Well," he said. "So what?"

"So what!" I exclaimed. "What do you mean, so what! I can't hear right. I'm, you know, I'm hard of hearing."

Mark reached for my hand. "Hey, it's okay," he said. "It won't be all that terrible. I mean, you'll get used to it."

"How can I get used to it?" I demanded. "They say I've even got to try wearing a hearing aid."

"You do?" Mark asked. Now he looked a little more concerned. "Wow! How bad is it, anyway — your hearing?"

"Bad enough. Mom wants to go into school and tell all my teachers I have to sit up in the front, but I won't let her. I can't stand it if everybody starts treating me differently."

"You've been so quiet lately," Mark mused. "A lot of times I thought you weren't quite following what people said. A couple months ago, when you kept sitting by yourself in the cafeteria and everything, I was really getting kind of worried. But you kept saying you were okay, and you started to act more normal again . . ."

"Act," I said dully. "It was all a big act. Now you know."

Mark's hand tightened over mine. "I know you're smart and fun and good at drama and lots of things," he said. "What difference does it make if you can't hear perfectly? If you wear a hearing aid, even? Nobody's perfect, right? Everybody's got something —"

"Oh, come off it," I said. I tried to pull my hand away. "You sound just like my father. That's the same lecture he's been giving me."

Mark let my hand go. He settled back into the corner of the couch. The reality was finally hitting him, I thought. He was stuck with a girl who was really weird. I remembered how Fred Margolis had joked about some guy with a girl friend whose ears stuck out. Mine didn't just stick out, they malfunctioned.

"Well, your dad's right," Mark said uncertainly. "Everybody's got crooked teeth or pimples or they're too fat or something."

"Well, not everybody is hard of hearing," I said. "I don't know one other person who wears a hearing aid except my old decrepit Aunt Dora."

That brought Mark to a halt. For a long minute he just sat there as if he couldn't think of anything else to say. I was doing this all wrong, I thought miserably. Mark was trying to tell me that it didn't really matter, that his feelings toward me didn't have to change. Why didn't I just go along with him, try to believe that it could be true?

But it was time to bring everything out into the open and get it over with. No more acting, no more pretenses.

"What caused it, anyway?" Mark asked finally.

"They don't know for sure. Maybe I was born with something the matter and lately it's been getting even worse."

"Well, see?" Mark said, brightening. "That just shows you. You never worried about all this when you didn't know about it. You were getting along fine. And you still are. You can just go on doing the things you've always done. People won't even have to know unless you tell them yourself."

"But you know," I said. I studied the flower pattern in the carpet. Were those round yellow ones supposed to be daisies?

"I'm glad you told me." Mark's voice dropped and I had to bend toward him to catch his words. "I hope you trust me when it's something important."

Suddenly tears burned my eyes. I turned my head and tried to brush them away. The last thing I needed now was to start crying.

"Well, of course I trust you," I said a little brusquely. "Why shouldn't I?"

Mark was thoughtful. "I don't know. But if you really trusted me how come you didn't tell me about this before? You've been having problems for a while now."

"It's not that I didn't trust you," I pleaded. "It's just that — how could I tell you? Even now I've got this awful feeling it's going to ruin everything." My voice broke and I tried to turn away again.

But Mark wouldn't let me escape. "I don't know what you're talking about," he said, taking my hand again. "Nothing's ruined. We're both the same as always."

Could he really mean it? I searched his face for some clue. Maybe it was just imagination, but I thought his eyes flickered away from my gaze.

"Don't make believe," I begged. "Don't say things you don't mean."

"I won't."

His arms slipped around me and he pulled me close to him. For a moment it was as though nothing had changed between us. I closed my eyes and felt him warm and real beside me.

But suppose he was only trying to make me feel better? Once he got away by himself he'd have a chance to think everything over. Then he'd start to feel sorry for me. Maybe he'd think of ways he could gingerly loosen the ties between us.

I straightened up, drawing away from him. "Well, I better not keep you. You said you had a lot of chemistry."

"Right." Mark stood up. "I guess I better get to it."

We went to the kitchen and Mark pulled on his raincoat. Drops of water still tumbled from the hem onto the linoleum. He really hadn't been here very long, but I felt worn out, and relieved at the same time. Relieved in a grim sort of way. Mark seemed relieved too, to be up and on his way. "Well, see you tomorrow," he said as I walked him to the door. "Meet me at our regular table for lunch, okay?"

"Okay," I said. "See you."

I waited for him to say the words that so many times had meant one final hug, a slow tender good-bye: *Parting is such sweet sorrow* . . . But they didn't come. I opened the door and Mark stepped out into the rain. For a few moments I watched him cross the lawn to his car, his shoulders hunched, his head bowed against the wind.

Then I stepped back inside and shut the door between us.

NINETEEN

I hadn't thought out in advance how I was going to break the news to Nancy. When I thought about it later I wished I hadn't told her at all. But one afternoon I missed the punch line of a joke she was trying to tell me, and after she repeated it two more times she exclaimed, "Oh, just forget it, all right?" And I said, "I can't hear you. I really don't hear all that well."

It took a minute or two for Nancy to realize that I wasn't just kidding. Then she overflowed with sympathy. She marveled that she had never realized before. She told me all about a friend of her mother's who wore a hearing aid concealed in her glasses frame. She kept asking what she could do for me, and she couldn't seem to grasp that I didn't need her to do anything but be herself.

As I should have expected, Nancy was so distressed by my news that she couldn't keep it to herself. She told Connie, who could hardly believe it either. And Connie related the story to

Mary Jo. Within two days practically everybody at school knew that I was now hearing impaired.

I could have stood the curious looks, and the way people fell silent when I approached as though they'd just been talking about me. I could almost have laughed at the way Barbara tried to speak to me with exaggerated lip movements across the table in the cafeteria.

But I couldn't endure the tension that had sprung up between Mark and me. We still ate lunch together, he drove me home most afternoons, and on Saturday nights we'd go to a movie or drop in at Joe's for pizza. But we didn't laugh the way we used to. The old feeling that Mark understood me without words seemed to have melted away. We almost never mentioned the problem with my hearing, but as the days turned into weeks I felt that it hung between us like a heavy black curtain.

When we were together I half expected him to flinch away if I touched him. If he turned away from me for a moment to speak to someone else I felt a pang of fear. He couldn't really want to be with me. He must prefer to be with other people, normal people who didn't require their own separate explanation of everything that was going on.

Still, whenever I dared to ask for reassurance, Mark insisted that nothing had changed. He was the same, I was the same. I had nothing to worry about, he would tell me.

I didn't want to talk about my ears too much. That might seem like dwelling on my handicap.

But there were things I would have liked to share with Mark sometimes, like the discoveries I was making with my new hearing aid.

Just as Dr. Crowell had predicted, the hearing aid was tiny. It fit neatly into place behind my right ear, and when I combed my hair down over it it was hidden completely.

And, although I hated to admit it, Dr. Crowell was also right when he said I would be amazed at the difference. I could actually hear the crackle of a newspaper from all the way across the room. I could hear the soft rumble of Minnie's purr like the motor of some tiny machine. Consonant sounds like S and P and T came through pure and distinct. Speech had a new sharpness. Words had never before had such clean, crisp edges.

I still only wore the hearing aid two hours a day to get accustomed to it. And that wasn't going to be easy. It didn't only help me hear things I wanted to hear. It amplified all the other sounds around me, too. It made a slamming door sound like a bomb going off, and turned the scraping of a chair into the shriek of a banshee. I didn't yet dare to try it at school.

I would have liked to talk with Mark about all of that. But he was making such a valiant attempt to conduct business as usual, to act as though my hearing loss had no effect on us at all, that I felt I ought to do the same.

He was waiting by my locker when I came up late after school one Friday afternoon. "Hey," he greeted me. "It's supposed to be a real nice day tomorrow. I was thinking, you want to go for a bike ride? Maybe we can go out to the quarry or something."

His smile sparkled. I could almost believe it was that special smile of his that I'd always felt was reserved for me.

"Oh, let's," I exclaimed. "We haven't done that for such a long time."

"Not since September when I got the car," Mark said. "We've been getting real lazy."

Maybe Mark really did mean it when he said my hearing didn't matter to him at all. Maybe all the tension and awkwardness between us had grown out of my own perverse imagination. "Well, I can sure use the exercise," I told him, returning his smile. "Let me just get a couple of books and we can get out of here for two whole days."

I twirled my locker combination and tugged at the handle, expecting the door to spring open as usual. But instead it only rattled.

"Darn," I muttered, and spun the dial again. Seventeen, twenty-four, eight. I knew I'd gotten the combination right, but still the door refused to open.

Mark gave it a try, but he had no better luck. When he yanked on the handle the door shuddered but wouldn't budge.

"What's the matter, your locker jammed?"

Neither of us had noticed Mary Jo. Now when I looked around she was trotting toward us, her frizzy hair bouncing, a tan straw purse swinging from her shoulder.

"It's jammed, all right," I said. "What a pain."

Naturally Mary Jo insisted on trying too, but she was no more successful than Mark or I had been. I gave the door a couple of solid kicks that set lockers shivering up and down the corridor.

Mary Jo came up close beside me. She bent her face to my ear and yelled, "I saw the custodian downstairs by the bookstore just now."

"Thanks," I said, stepping away quickly. "You don't have to shout, you know. If I'd had my hearing aid on you'd have blasted me to Kingdom Come."

"I was just trying to help," Mary Jo said, looking injured.

"I'll run down and try to find the janitor," I said. "Maybe he can figure this out."

I half expected Mark to come with me. But instead he said, "I'll meet you back here. I just want to run over to my locker for my sweater."

Mary Jo was right. One of the custodians, Mr. de Crespo, was buffing the floor just beyond the school store. He was the youngest and nicest member of the maintenance crew. He grinned at me and offered to come straight upstairs and take care of everything.

When we got back upstairs Mark and Mary Jo stood in the hall just where I had left them. And Mark hadn't gone to his locker, either. I noticed right away he still didn't have his sweater.

They were talking, standing close together, but they broke off before I got near enough to hear what they were saying. "Wow, that was quick," Mark said. I wondered if he'd hoped I would be gone longer.

We all stood in silence watching Mr. de

Crespo at work. Humming to himself he spun the combination. Just as he pulled on the handle he delivered a sharp kick to the bottom of the door. "Open, sesame," he commanded, and the door flew open as if by magic.

"Hey, thanks," I exclaimed. "How did you do that? You make it look so easy."

"Maybe I ought to become a safe-cracker," Mr. de Crespo said. "There'd be a lot more money in it."

I glanced over at Mark and Mary Jo, ready to share the joke with them. But they didn't seem to have heard it. Mary Jo was whispering something to Mark, but when he saw me looking at them he put his finger to his lips. It was all over in an instant, but I knew what I had seen.

Mr. de Crespo swaggered off, whistling. Numbly I searched through my locker and fished out the books I needed. Mary Jo said she was in a hurry, so we said good-bye to her and went on over to Mark's locker.

I managed to wait until I was sure Mary Jo was out of earshot. Then I turned to Mark and demanded, "What were you guys talking about back there?"

Mark shrugged. "Nothing special. Why?"

"You seemed pretty involved in it, whatever it was."

"We did?" Mark got his sweater out of his locker and draped it over his arm. He sorted through his books.

"Yeah, you did. Anyway, I thought you said you were going to your locker while I went downstairs. You were up here talking the whole time I was gone." Why was I pursuing this? Probably it was nothing. But no, I hadn't imagined it. They had been talking to each other, low and intent, leaving me on the outside. Maybe Mary Jo was interested in Mark. Maybe she thought she had a chance with him now. And from what I'd seen, Mark wasn't doing much to discourage her.

"I couldn't hear what you were saying," I plunged on, unable to stop myself. "But you sure looked chummy."

Mark banged his locker shut and turned to stare at me. "What are you talking about? We were just standing there waiting while . . ."

"You were whispering about something. I saw you. You cut it out as soon as you knew I was watching." My voice rose. "What's so great about her, except that she can hear? I never in my whole life would have thought you'd want to hang around with somebody like her, like Mary Jo!"

"You're crazy! You're out of your mind!"

But it was too late now. The words just kept coming. "If you weren't stuck with me you could have whatever girl you want. But you don't know how to dump someone that's practically deaf. Well, you don't have to stick with me just because you feel sorry for me . . ."

"Jody, will you cut it out?"

". . . if you want to call it quits, just have the decency to be straight with me, okay? Just do me that favor, will you? That's all, just —"

"I don't believe this!" Mark exclaimed. "Whoever said anything about — what do you think I am, anyway? You really think I'm that dumb, that shallow, that I'd just drop you on account of your ears?"

"I didn't say you were dumb or shallow," I said. "I'm just being realistic. There's no use pretending. I know how you really feel."

Suddenly Mark's face seemed to harden. "So this is what I get," he said. "I've been bending over backward trying to be nice to you —"

"Yes, that's just it," I cried. "Trying to be nice to me. You've really got to try though, because it's not all that easy with somebody like me —"

"No, not the way you're acting," Mark said. "I don't know why I even bother. I wanted to show you that nothing was changed, but I guess I had it all wrong. I'll see you around."

What had I done? Mark was turning, walking away from me. He was right, I was acting crazy!

"Mark!" I cried. "I didn't mean it. Where are you going?"

"I don't know. Just leave me alone, will you?"

I felt as if my heart had stopped beating. I could hardly breathe as I stood there watching him go. I'd expected something like this to happen all along. But I still wasn't prepared for it now that the worst had come.

I hadn't meant to get angry at Mark. What was the matter with me? I'd been almost happy just a few minutes ago.

Suddenly I came to life again. "Mark!" I cried, dashing after him down the hall. "Mark, wait!"

But he had already disappeared into the stairwell. I flung open the door and gazed down over the railing at the flight of empty stairs. He must have run all the way down. Now he was gone. And even if I could catch up with him, what could I say now? I had ruined everything.

"Oh, Mark," I sobbed, but no one was there to hear me.

TWENTY

I hadn't really cried since that afternoon when Kim sat in my room and asked me point-blank if I could hear all right. I'd gone through all the appointments with Dr. Crowell in a kind of daze, being brave, assuring everyone around me that I was taking it all in stride. Somehow I had plowed my way through the past weeks, putting on smiles when I needed them. But now as I began to run, tears clouded my vision. By the time I flung myself through the door of the girls' washroom the tide of sobbing had overtaken me.

The girls' room was empty. I collapsed onto a chair and my sobs echoed back from the tiled walls. I couldn't pretend even to myself that I was getting along fine. "I can't stand it!" I moaned, covering my face with my hands. "I can't stand it! It's not fair!"

Mark was gone. I had lost him forever now. And I had to go through life wearing a hearing aid, and I just didn't know how I was going to live with it.

But as desperate as I felt, pretty soon I began to wonder what I would say if someone came in and found me sitting there. It was bad enough that people knew I had a hearing loss. But if anyone found me in here, weeping like the heroine from some soap opera, they'd say I was losing my mind, too. After a while my sobs turned to sniffles, and the longer I sat on my rickety wooden chair the more urgently I needed to get myself up and moving again.

Shakily I got to my feet at last. My face stared back, red and puffy from the mirror above the row of sinks. I dashed cold water onto my cheeks and tugged a comb through my hair and hoped I could make myself look presentable. The walk home would do me good. By the time I opened the front door Mom wouldn't be able to tell that I'd been crying.

As I stepped out into the hall again I almost imagined that Mark would be standing by the door, waiting to tell me that everything was still all right between us. I would say I was sorry, that I'd been acting like an idiot, and we'd walk out to the parking lot hand in hand . . .

But Mark wasn't there. The hall stretched ahead of me, long and empty. Mark was gone. I couldn't tell him I was sorry, it was too late for that.

I don't remember descending the stairs. I just kept putting one foot in front of the other, my mind vacant. But suddenly, as I emerged into the first-floor corridor, a thought pierced my numbness. Mark and I wouldn't go bicycling together tomorrow. Maybe we would never go bicycling together again. The realization jolted me to a standstill. This was the real meaning of what had happened. There would be no more phone calls, no drives in Mark's Volkswagen bug, no games of backgammon. No more smiles flashing between us. It was all over.

I swayed and sagged against the wall. I stood there in the silent corridor, staring into space, the cruel truth resounding inside my head.

"Jody, are you all right?"

The voice came from very close behind me. I whirled around and found myself face to face with Mrs. Ikeda.

"Oh, sure," I said. But my voice came out cracked and brittle from too much crying. "Hi, I didn't hear you coming."

"I don't mean to pry," Mrs. Ikeda said, "but you don't look all right. Is there anything I can do?"

It was my old familiar cue. My worn old lines rushed to my lips: *No, don't worry, I'm perfectly fine . . .*

But somehow I knew I couldn't convince her. And I didn't have the strength to try. "No, you can't do anything really," I heard myself say. "It's just — oh, Mark and I just had a big fight . . ." My voice broke. Somehow I still hadn't run out of tears.

"Oh, no," Mrs. Ikeda sighed. "I'm sorry."

Even then I could have walked away. But I couldn't hold back the words. "It was all my fault," I cried. "He was trying to be nice to me but I just wouldn't let him. I ruined everything."

174

Mrs. Ikeda set down her briefcase as though she was prepared to be here for a while. "Oh, I bet it's not really that bad," she began. "You're upset now, but —"

"It's worse than you think," I rushed on. "I can't stand him feeling sorry for me, and — oh, never mind. You don't want to listen to all this."

"Well, I'm not in a hurry, if you feel like telling me about it. What on earth makes you think Mark would feel sorry for you?"

"Because of my hearing," I said almost impatiently. "He kept saying it didn't make any difference to him, but —"

Mrs. Ikeda held up her hand to stop me. "Wait a second, wait a second. What do you mean, because of your hearing?"

By now I felt as though the whole world must know. But just because Mary Jo's tales sped from mouth to mouth through the student body that didn't mean that the teachers had all heard the news yet. But now that I'd gone this far I'd have to explain it myself.

"I just found out that I don't hear too well," I said. I looked at the floor. "Like I'm supposed to start wearing a hearing aid and all that stuff."

"Mrs. Ikeda's eyes grew wide and round. Not even Mary Jo had stared at me in such open amazement.

"I'm not deaf," I said, bristling. "It's no big deal, just —"

"When did you find this out?" Mrs. Ikeda leaned toward me as though she was eager for every grisly detail.

"A couple weeks ago." I turned away. "I better

go now. It's pretty late." This would teach me not to go around confiding in people.

"No, wait a minute." Mrs. Ikeda held out a restraining hand. "I don't want you to get the wrong idea. It's just that, well, I'm very interested in this because I have the same problem myself."

In the first moment or two I didn't quite grasp what she meant. Even when I replayed her words inside my head I couldn't believe what I had heard. My ears must have been deceiving me again.

"I've had a hearing aid since I was twelve," Mrs. Ikeda went on. "I hardly think about it anymore, I'm so used to it."

Now it was my turn to stare. "You!" I exclaimed. "How can you? You're a teacher! You're the drama teacher!"

"Oh, being a teacher doesn't stop me from wearing a hearing aid. Or does it work the other way, wearing a hearing aid doesn't stop me from being a teacher?"

I didn't know what to say. But I watched, fascinated, as Mrs. Ikeda brushed back her hair. Sure enough, a tiny plastic box perched behind her left ear.

"Since you were twelve?" I repeated. "Then you went all through school and got a job and directed plays and everything — how do you do it?"

"Oh, about the same way you do things, I suppose," she laughed. "You acted in a play, so why shouldn't I direct plays?"

"And nobody ever guesses," I breathed. "People see you every single day and it never occurs to anybody."

Mrs. Ikeda shrugged. "Most of the other teachers know. Maybe some of the kids, too. It's not exactly a deep dark secret."

"Hey," I exclaimed, "when you were getting us to project you always used to say you were the deaf lady with the hearing aid sitting in the back row."

"You thought I was kidding, right?"

"Yes," I said. "But if I'd only known! All that time we were doing *A Doll's House* I was so worried about my hearing and trying to hide all the problems from everybody. And I was sure if you found out you'd never let me have the part."

"What would you call that, dramatic irony?" But she grew suddenly serious. "Sometimes people really do try to tell you you can't do something because of your hearing. I almost didn't get hired for this teaching job, as a matter of fact. I had to fight for it. But I showed them I hadn't had any trouble doing my practice teaching, so they gave me a chance."

"Do a lot of people treat you differently when they find out?" I asked. "I mean, like you were weird or something?" What right did I have to ask her all these questions about her personal life? But I couldn't stop myself. There were so many things I had to know.

"Well, some people just never worry about it at all. And some people can't ever seem to forget it. But most people, well, at first they aren't too sure what to say, but pretty soon they just get used to it." She lifted up her hair to show me her hearing aid.

I'd always liked and admired Mrs. Ikeda. She was one of those women who seemed to have everything — intelligence, looks, a husband, a career she obviously enjoyed. It hardly seemed possible — but that little plastic box next to her ear was proof.

"Doesn't it drive you crazy when the class is making a racket?" I asked. "I can't stand much noise. And when I've got my hearing aid on it's even worse."

"When they start getting noisy I make them knock it off right away," Mrs. Ikeda said. "I guess it creates the impression I'm super strict. But really I'm just doing it in self-defense. By the way, how long did you say you've been using a hearing aid?"

"Just about two weeks now. I haven't worn it at school yet. I don't know if it's going to help me much really."

"You'll get used to it," she assured me. She added quickly, "I know, I know, that's what everybody says, right? But it really is true. And if you don't, then maybe the aid they gave you to try out isn't right for you. Just tell the audiologist you want to try out a different one if you're not happy. The main thing is you've got to hear as much as you can. That way you won't feel left out of things."

"Do you read lips?" I asked. There was no end to my parade of questions.

"Some," she said. "I picked up a bit on my own, and then one summer I took a lipreading course over at the Hearing Center. It really helped a lot."

"The audiologist wanted me to take something like that," I said. "But I thought it sounded like a dumb idea."

"Well, you might want to try it some day. It helps me a lot, and it can be a lot of fun. We were at a party last Saturday night and I saw this woman looking at my dress. Then she said something to her friend and from across the room I could read her friend's lips. She said, 'Oh, no, I know where she got it. I saw that dress over at the Bargain Basement.'"

We both laughed. If I'd been able to lipread, I thought, maybe I would have known what Mark and Mary Jo were talking about.

But I wasn't ready to think about Mark and Mary Jo again. "Is it very hard to learn?" I asked. "I bet it would be neat, especially in places like the cafeteria where it's real noisy, or on stage to be sure I was following all the lines."

"Some people are easy to read. Some people are about impossible. Like guys with moustaches —forget it!"

Suddenly I caught a flicker of movement at the far end of the corridor. Mr. de Crespo came into view around the corner. His lips were pursed as though he was whistling, but at that distance I could only hear the clang of his mop handle against the metal pail he was carrying.

"What is it with you people, you love this

place?" he demanded as he drew nearer. "You're not going to make me throw you out, are you?"

Mrs. Ikeda glanced at her watch. "I suppose I really better be getting home," she said. "My husband doesn't mind getting dinner ready, but he does like me to show up to eat it while it's still hot."

What must her husband be like, I wondered. How did he feel about a woman who wore a hearing aid? Well, it couldn't have mattered to him very much, because he'd gone ahead and married her.

"I shouldn't be keeping you so long," I said to Mrs. Ikeda as Mr. de Crespo sauntered off, his pail clanging. "It's just there are so many things I want to ask you about. I can't tell you how much better I feel just talking to you, knowing I'm not the only one."

"Listen," she said. "Any time you feel like talking, just drop by my homeroom after school. I really mean it."

"I will," I promised. "Boy, I wish I'd known all along that you had a hearing problem. It makes me feel like, well, maybe it's not so awful. It doesn't stop you from doing anything you want to."

Mrs. Ikeda picked up her briefcase. Together we started across the foyer. "You know," she said, "maybe I have been a little bit secretive about it, more than I realized. I keep joking about being the lady with the hearing aid. But sometimes it really might be easier if more people knew it's true. And," she added with a twinkle, "what good is all this hearing if people don't talk?"

"That's the truth," I said. "I guess I've gotten into all kinds of trouble lately by not talking."

We pushed our way out through the front door into the soft May afternoon. I walked with Mrs. Ikeda as far as the faculty parking lot. "Let me know how you're doing with your hearing aid," she said. "And give my regards to Mark, okay?"

I threw her a startled glance but she was smiling almost slyly. Had she forgotten that Mark and I had had a fight, that maybe he would never speak to me again? Or was she trying to tell me something.

"Okay," I promised. "I will."

TWENTY-ONE

I called Mom from the pay phone out in front
of the school. "I'm going to be late," I told her.
"I've got to see Mark about something."

"You're all right?" Concern rose in Mom's
voice, that anxiety that was there so often now
when she spoke to me.

"Yeah," I said. "I'm fine. It's just that I've got
to talk to him about something important."

It was a long walk over to Mark's house, but
that gave me plenty of time to think. Over and
over I rehearsed speeches inside my head, some
woeful and apologetic, others light and funny,
trying to pull some shred of humor out of our sit-
uation. Maybe Mark would refuse to see me.
Maybe he'd slam the door in my face. But I had
to make him listen to me. There was so much I
needed to tell him.

It was a warm spring evening but I felt suddenly cold all over as I stood on the doormat,
waiting for someone to answer the bell. For a

long minute no one seemed to stir inside. I could turn and run, and Mark would never have to know that I had come after him like this.

No, I told myself sternly. I had to tell Mark that I had been wrong, and I had to tell him now. I lifted my hand and pressed the doorbell again.

At last someone pulled the door open. "Oh, it's you," said Mark's twelve-year-old sister Lisa, peering out at me. "We're just eating dinner."

"Oh, I'm sorry." It had never occurred to me that I might show up at a bad time. I just had to see Mark. Time wasn't important.

Lisa opened the door a few inches wider. "Well, you might as well come in," she said. "We're having succotash. You want mine?"

"No, thanks." I shuddered at the thought of sitting down with Mark's family, making polite conversation as if this were just an ordinary visit. My feet were rooted to the rubber doormat. "I'll just wait out here till Mark —"

"Lisa, who — oh, Jody." And then, miraculously, Mark replaced his sister in the doorway. For a few seconds we stood in silence, eying each other warily.

I spoke first. "I wanted to talk to you. Can I just wait out here?"

Mark stepped out onto the porch and shut the door after him. "What's up?" he asked shortly.

All my speeches had deserted me. "Listen," I stammered. "I just came to say — to tell you — I'm sorry."

I thought a glimmer of warmth passed across Mark's face. But I couldn't be sure. "Sorry for what?" he asked, looking straight at me.

"For making such a scene back there this afternoon. It was stupid of me. It was really paranoid of me to think you and Mary Jo were, you know . . ."

I struggled to read Mark's expression. "Oh, that's not all that important," he said finally. "I should have been more careful to talk so you could hear me."

Was Mark going to turn it around and say that the whole problem had been his fault? I couldn't let him do that to himself. "Look," I said. "It's not just this afternoon. All the way over here I was realizing that I haven't been very nice at all lately. Since I told you about my hearing. No, it started way before that, even. I guess I've been giving you an awful lot of hassles."

Mark thrust his hands into his pockets. "You could say so. We just haven't been understanding each other for a pretty long time now."

He was telling me that it was too late. I had finally pushed him too far and now he couldn't forgive me.

"I was so afraid I was going to lose you," I said desperately. "I didn't want you to know about my hearing. Then when I finally had to tell you I was so sure it was going to ruin everything."

"I tried to get that idea out of your head," Mark reminded me. "I kept trying to show you that I felt the same as before. It's not me that changed, it's you. You don't accept me anymore."

"No!" I cried. "That's not true. How can you say —"

Behind us the door popped open and Mark's mother leaned out. "Oh, there you are. Why don't you two come in and have some dessert?"

"No, not right now," Mark said. "We're going for a walk."

There was a scrap of hope then. At least he was willing to walk with me, and to go on talking. And he motioned for me to leave my books on the porch. That meant I'd have to come back to the house with him, too.

But we were silent for almost half a block. We passed a gang of kids playing ball on a wide green lawn. We sidestepped the swinging arm of a sprinkler that doused the sidewalk.

At last I pulled my scattered thoughts together and began, "You say I don't accept you anymore. I guess that's how it seems to you. But I know how most boys feel about any girl that's different. They figure she's weird. So I just kept waiting for you to do things that would show you didn't want to be with me."

"I know," Mark said. He looked away across the quiet street. I had to strain for his next words. "That's what hurt."

His words stabbed me. I stopped, stood perfectly still. And as we stood there on the sidewalk looking at each other, the word that flashed into my mind was *unwavering*. Mark had never changed. His loyalty toward me had never weakened. And still I hadn't trusted him.

"I'm sorry." My words weren't much more than

a whisper. "All this time I never looked at it that way. I guess I just kept thinking about myself, what *I* was going through, what *I* was afraid of. I just never thought of how I was —"

"Underestimating me?" Mark finished with the hint of a wry grin.

"Yeah," I said. "That's what I mean."

We started to walk again. At the end of the street we turned off the sidewalk and followed a set of rusted railroad tracks through a field of tall grass. I felt miserable at the way I'd been treating Mark. I'd make it up to him if only he would give me another chance. But I couldn't guess what was in his mind as we scuffed through the gravel beside the tracks.

At last Mark turned to me again. "I guess it is true that a lot of guys, and girls too, get freaked out at first if somebody's different. I don't know why, exactly. But I know that not everybody is like that. Because I really don't give a damn whether you wear a hearing aid. Your ears were never what attracted me to you in the first place."

I laughed a little shakily. "You're too good to be true," I cried, and flung my arms around him. "I don't deserve you. Really I don't."

Mark tilted my face up to his. "Hey, it's good to see you smiling. Lately I hardly ever see a real smile from you."

I smiled. And Mark bent and kissed me lightly on the lips.

"You know," I said after a while, when we had turned to retrace our steps, "I found out the most incredible thing this afternoon. I ran into Mrs.

Ikeda, and you'll never guess what? She wears a hearing aid, too."

"Well, what's so incredible about that?" Mark asked. "Some of my best friends have hearing aids."

"But somebody like Mrs. Ikeda? Seriously, who'd ever think it?"

"You know how it is when you first learn a new word? You start seeing it more and more often when you read. I bet you'll keep meeting more and more people with hearing aids the same way."

"I never really felt like I could talk to anyone about it before, and have them understand," I went on. "But with her I couldn't stop asking questions. Just knowing she's been through the same thing makes me feel a lot more normal." I kicked a stone ahead of me and watched it bounce into the gutter. "If I hadn't run into her I don't know if I'd have had the guts to come look for you tonight."

"Don't worry," Mark said. "I was going to drop over at your place right after dinner."

"You mean you really weren't planning to get together with Mary Jo tonight?" I tried to say it lightly, but I still wanted that final reassurance.

"No," Mark said. "She's just not my type. She was saying something dumb about how well you were managing in spite of your handicap and I figured you'd get mad if you heard any of it, so I was trying to hush her up."

"I should have guessed," I said. "Knowing her — and knowing you."

We had reached Mark's street again. "You left your books on our porch," he said. "Want to come in for some dessert?"

"Sure," I said. "Sounds great."

"And, oh, by the way, tomorrow do you still want to go for a bike ride?"

"Oh, Mark. Do I ever!"

Mark grabbed my hand and together we ran up the sidewalk toward his house. I guess I must have been beaming. And Mark's face shone with that special smile that was always meant for me alone.